Praise for *Here They Come:*

"This is a hell of a book. You might not be able to finish *Here They Come* in one sitting, but it will haunt you till you do. What detail! What characters! I can imagine both Jane Austen and Raymond Carver poring over this masterly novel."

—Frank McCourt, author of *Angela's Ashes*

"Yannick Murphy is a uniquely talented writer who manages to turn everything on its head and make dark, funny, shocking, and beautiful prose out of the detritus of growing up poor, fatherless, and cockeyed. She is fearless."

—Lily Tuck, author of *The News from Paraguay,* winner of the 2004 National Book Award

"*Here They Come* is a unique combination of rare linguistic lyricism with brutal and brilliant prose. It is an unrelenting portrait of family, terrifying for its honesty, its willingness to be ugly and elegant. Haunting."

—A. M. Homes, author of *This Book Will Save Your Life*

"Told by a precocious unnamed thirteen-year-old girl who bends spoons with her mind, Murphy's gorgeous third book of fiction recounts the story of a poor family's coming-of-age in 1970s New York. In thick, poetic prose that edges toward stream of consciousness and is peppered with slightly surreal details, Murphy creates a world as magical and harrowing as the struggle to come to grips with maturity."

—*Publishers Weekly* (starred review)

"Yannick Murphy creates a narrator with a unique, sometimes shocking perspective. Murphy's startling language and imagery accumulate great power as they hurtle toward the reader."

—*People*

"From deep in the trenches of family dysfunctionality, this story magnifies the weird but absorbing life of a girl coping with a broken home [A] readable work . . . at once funny an *brary Journal*

HERE THEY COME

YANNICK MURPHY

Grove/McSweeney's
New York/San Francisco

First published in 2006 by McSweeney's Books, San Francisco

Published simultaneously in Canada
Printed in the United States of America

FIRST PAPERBACK EDITION

Library of Congress Cataloging-in-Publication Data

ISBN-10: 0-8021-4319-9
ISBN-13: 978-0-8021-4319-8

Grove Press
an imprint of Grove/Atlantic, Inc.
841 Broadway
New York, NY 10003

McSweeny's Books
849 Valencia St.
San Francisco, CA

Distributed by Publishers Group West

www.groveatlantic.com

07 08 09 10 11 12   10 9 8 7 6 5 4 3 2 1

For Wicca, a German shepherd; Jochen, a neighbor; Tom and Polly, grocery store clerks; Mario, an elevator man; some of my schoolteachers, but not all of them; and the Mother of Eleven.

And for Jeff, who, in case you were wondering, has a direct line now to the surf gods.

Many thanks to Judy Heiblum for being relentless, Eli Horowitz for being a real editor, and Nicole Bettauer for being a believer.

Here come the hot dog men. Fuck, if they aren't all foreign, all coming from lands with camels and beaches with black volcanic ash for sand or lands with wives with scarves up to the eyes, lands where love is through a hole in the bedsheet, lands where marriages are on hilltops, and goats, bell-necked, graze nearby. They are silent down the avenue except for the wheels of their carts and the slosh of the water their long skinny hot dogs float in. So early down the avenue there are hardly any cars, and they own the lanes, pushing their carts down the middle wearing sometimes three sweaters, their arms bulging in nubby hand-knitted yarns, their shoes sometimes not shoes, just sandals worn with socks, their hair greased or just greasy, the dandruff held tight behind bars of coarse strands of thick prickly hair at the napes of their cross-hatched necks.

I see them coming down the avenue from my fire escape, their cart umbrellas folded in. Their slow walk is like an amble through a still sleeping village alongside a donkey-drawn wooden-wheeled cart loaded with bundles of sticks for starting small fires.

I know the one walking past the Charlie Bar across the street. He is named John. He gives me a Hershey from the bin at the bottom that stores the spongy buns. In summer I sit on his lap when it is slow, and morning, and eat the Hershey while I feel his fingers creeping up my waist and to my tits. Meanwhile, the hot dogs boil, the sauerkraut warms, and the sodas cool on ice.

John doesn't have front teeth. He says it's from eating rocks baked in bread where he comes from. He takes pictures of me with a camera he wears around his neck and shows me them developed. Bad pictures where the sun is behind me and I'm a whoosh of bright light, or under a park bush, too dark to be seen, maybe just my leg on the dirt that is patted-down park dirt, run over by rats at night and where minty gum wrapper is thrown throughout the day.

At home I sit on the toilet looking at the water heater where Louisa has drawn in cray-pas faces of the boys she likes at school. We all say she could be the artist. She has sketched me with the cat curled in my lap. It's winter and so cold in the house the cats are always barnacled to us. When we're sitting in chairs they're on our laps and when we walk across the house they trot after us, waiting for us to sit again. When we sleep they lie on our heads and our backs and our feet and if we roll over or kick they grab onto us with their claws and dig in through the blankets, scared to be tossed from our warmth.

* * *

In the morning, when our mother wakes, she is the first to take the stick end of the plunger and break the ice in the toilet so she can pee without it splashing back. In our beds we hear the chink-chink of the ice cracking.

My father lives uptown with a short blonde he found on a set, porno or not, we don't know. I looked through her drawers once and held up her lace bras and put one on and then my father called me from the other room and we went sledding down Dog Hill, me wearing the slut's black bra number on top of Jody and Jody on top of Louisa and then we fell over at the end of the ride and bent the sled's runner, our weight too much for the metal.

My father's drinking and telling us how stupid his slut is because she thinks the sun is not a star. She's not here because it's Christmas Eve and we're spending it alone with him in his apartment and she's with her brothers somewhere out in New Jersey with a big fir tree they cut down off their parents' land for their Tannenbaum. I'm beginning to think his slut's smart, that maybe she's right and the sun is not a star but it's a planet and this adds to my choices of where I could go when I leave this world and I feel I've expanded my horizons and found the far west. My Christmas present is a doll with red hair and a plaid skirt but I give her an Indian name and call her Tenderleaf Teresa. The first thing I do after I unwrap her

3

is cut her hair. I think it needs a trim. My brother laughs and tells me her hair won't grow back. The cab ride home is like a rocket trip, we hit every green light and there are no other cars because it's Christmas Eve. I've never gone anywhere so fast in New York in all my life.

I imagine I'm my father's slut and I'm in New Jersey in a room that smells like Christmas and there's snow outside on the ground lit up by moonlight and blond brothers in oxfords singing the first Noel and slightly swaying on the backs of their heels while they've got their arms around each other and around me. I imagine I'm his slut and I'm happy and it's Christmas and I'm with blond brothers and the sun is a planet, and the phone is ringing and ringing somewhere in my parents' country home and it's my tanked sugar daddy trying to call after his four kids have left and now he wants me and he wants a little of my Hallmark Christmas, a piece of my pumpkin pie, a feel of glossy gift wrap and a whiff of the pine and a taste of what's nutmegged and powdered sugary and meant well, the crèche holy and blessed. It's my scab-headed Cal, my drunk drunk on the huge-size Gallo they sell for mixing vats of sangria he drinks alone after his kids have scampered back downtown.

"Let it ring," I say to my blond brothers, and we do and we continue with our Christmas and our swaying and watch ourselves armlinked and distorted in our red and green bulb tree ornaments as we sing.

My brother plays guitar in clubs till late at night and is hardly ever home during the day. Sometimes I wake in the night and hear him when he has come back walking through the house, his guitar case hitting up against a chair our mother forgot to move. She makes a path for him before she goes to sleep, like she's clearing room for a dance floor, and I go to bed thinking I can't sleep, something's going to happen, people will come over and turn on music and there will be a party and laughter, but nothing does happen, my mother just comes to bed, sleeps alongside me and cries the way she always does.

John lifts me up onto a metal box bolted to the street lamp and as he does, he slides his hands up high under my knit top. I like it up high. I can see the whole park, a juggler or band or preacher at work in the pit of the fountain when it's not on. The metal box is warm and it clicks when the light turns from red to green. John passes me up a hot dog and my soda and I watch a taxi cut off a car. The taxi driver starts yelling and the two men get out and stop traffic and all the while the metal box I'm on clicks while the light turns from red to green.

It ends with a horse cop on the scene. I can see his stallion. I think he's trying to look at me, but then I see him rolling one eye so far back it looks like what he's trying to see is inside his head.

Of course I get all the hot dogs I ever want. John tries to get me on onion, but I like them plain, no mustard or anything. I drink orange soda or sometimes cream. I sit on the curb and eat. John kisses me goodbye. He says it's all he wants. I request the Hershey with almonds next time, nuts in things are my thing, I tell him, they're my bag. He laughs, he says where he comes from hard-boiled eggs are baked into loaves of braided bread.

"What about the shells?" I want to know. "All that fucking sharpness in your teeth," I say.

I curse all the time, or maybe it's just "fuck" I always say. Fuck, I think it too, fuck, bread must have been all the hot dog men ever ate in their countries.

My mother says shit in French all the time. Merde when the electric gets cut. Merde when the candlestick wax drips onto her clothes. Merde when the gas gets cut too and we eat cold sandwiches each night for dinner. Merde in her sleep while I lie next to her in bed, merde a scream in a string of other French I do not understand. Maybe all the sleep-talking is why our father left.

* * *

An angel woke me when my sister was sleeping too close to the old space heater and the flame went off and the whole house smelled like gas. I tugged at my sister's shoulder and tugged and tugged and finally her eyes opened and she told me to leave her alone, she was sleeping. The angel was floating above my head when it happened and she kept calling my name and I didn't want to wake up either, but she was fucking persistent, this angel, and so I turned off the gas and saved everyone's life.

I'm the one who shops and I've got ten bucks for two days to feed the five of us. Polly at the A & P knows I've only ever got ten bucks and she says "How ya doin, Smitty?" Then she passes through a bunch of my items without ringing them up and gives me a wink. I even come home with change. Tom does it too, but his nose is huge and red and usually has a ripe white pimple on it, so I don't like to stand on his line, but like I said, he'll do it too and not charge me for some items and wink when he's packing the bags and call me Smitty.

Two weeks after Easter the store's chocolate hasn't all sold so Polly and Tom throw leftover chocolate bunny rabbits into my bag after I've already paid. My mother says Polly and Tom are saints and shakes her head and counts out loud in French the change I give her back and takes a bite out of my stale chocolate rabbit's ear. She hands it back to me one-eared and

I pick out the candy sugar eye and eat it and then put the rabbit back in its box and up on a shelf. Missing an eye, now it's not able to look out its plastic window at me and my mother doing whatever we do in our house.

It's summer now and so hot we've got maggots living on ooze that leaks from the garbage we keep piled in bags in our house. We've got no private pickup and we've been cited for leaving a bag here and there in the metal baskets on street corners.

"Merde," my mother says and sprays the maggots with so much bug spray the maggots float off in little rivulets that head for the front of our house because our floors are slanted, and I feel in my sleep I could be tipped and slide off my bed right out of the window and onto the avenue.

Fuck, when it gets too hot I bring my mattress out on the fire escape and sleep through the night with the sound of the Charlie Bar music across the street being played from a juke-box. Facedown in the early morning I look over the fire escape at the tops of the heads of the hot dog men trundling their carts and I spit, hoping the wind will carry my spit and land on them.

We are leaning over our father's shoulder, our long hair

hanging down by his cheeks, the ends resting on the cotton cloth of his button-down shirt. He is sitting at the table and sketching Mickey Mouse on a pad of paper. We often ask him to sketch Mickey Mouse. It's one of the tricks we know he can do for us. We are always amazed. His magic marker moves quickly and the sketches look just like Mickey. Standing beside him we notice that our father's bald head looks like a relief map. There are scabs on it from hitting low doorways, where stray nails have cut, where sun has cooked the skin. Moles spread out like lake shapes and scars are craters and scattered strands of a half dozen hairs still hanging on are some kind of dune grass blowing in the wind. Wine too has formed red blotches on his head.

He sways and loses balance while standing in his summer rental telling me again his slut doesn't know the sun is a star and how stupid she is. She is smart and she is upstairs already in their bed, away from him and his drunkenness, and I am still with him in the kitchen wanting him to sit down, he is making me seasick as he moves from side to side. I go to bed and I swear the moon is the sun, it's so red.

In the morning he is at work on the Steenbeck, rewinding and fast-forwarding all day sounding like Oz, the land of the munchkins, only the picture on his screen is of military men.

"Values," one man on the screen says, and my father rewinds.

"Values are," the man says, frontwards and backwards, and I walk through the house all morning and wait for the rest of the sentence but my father never gets there. He stops the Steenbeck, the screen frozen on the man's open mouth, and gets up from his chair, goes to the kitchen and makes a sandwich. In the kitchen my father asks me where his slut is and I tell him she's gone on safari because I saw her pack water and a towel in her beach bag. He nods his head and makes me a sandwich of cucumber and mayonnaise and says on a hot summer's day you don't need anything else to eat. But after the sandwich I'm still hungry and eat crackers when he goes back to his Steenbeck.

"Values are an indescribable..." is what I get the rest of the afternoon. The next morning my father tells me his slut thinks it's time I go home. I run up the metal steps and onto the train. I don't bother to take a seat for the longest time, I look down in the space made where the two cars connect as we speed over the gravel-strewn ground that just looks like a blur.

Coming through the dark of Penn Station takes such a long time I could be in some other land where it's night, and from the train wheels all I hear is the word, "values" frontwards and backwards and over and over again through the darkened land.

At home I am Sadie Somebody stripteasing on a tabletop for my sisters, undoing buttons of my rosebud pajamas. They are all laughing, and the dog is barking because I'm up too high and she wants me to get down the same way when we're out in the water she bites at our necks to get a hold and tow us back to shore or the way she herds us away from the cars when we walk down the avenue. Fuck, a dog like that and who needs a mother or a father? But to her own she was unfit and ate them, leaving blood and fur in the pen after they were born.

My mother sleeps the sleep of the accident dead, not in deepness but in the way her arms are flung, like a person found on the side of the road thrown from a car, her arms twisted up around her head, her mouth agape, her body naked. When it's summer it is so hot in our house she calls us tomatoes and the skylights make it a greenhouse. She says we are the five little tomatoes and how they grew and I tell her the book's name is *The Five Little Peppers and How They Grew* and she says she doesn't feel like a pepper but more like a tomato, bruised and caving in and on its way to seed.

I go to the park and I see the cop on his stallion again, and the stallion looks at me while I'm scratching my name with a pen into a park bench seat. The cop doesn't care, but the stallion keeps looking at me like if he didn't have the cop on his back he'd come right over and strike me down with his hooves. I give the stallion the finger, but only to his chestnut haunch when he's already passed me by.

At home late that night our mother is drunk, hanging onto the bedpost with her shoes in her hand, laughing, saying she and her friends drove to Coney Island and swam in the waves. She gets into bed next to me still in her clothes and falls asleep smelling of ocean. Toward morning her liquor wears off and I hear crying and it isn't until then I feel things are back to normal and I can really get some sleep.

My mother has forgotten to clear a path for my brother. He comes through crashing his guitar against a cherrywood straightback chair and from inside the case you can hear a few notes twang. He keeps walking and his guitar hits another chair and then another one.

"Godfuckingdammit," he says and he drops the guitar and picks up one of the chairs and throws it across the house and then he picks up the chair again and goes to the back door and opens it and throws the chair down five flights of stairs where its legs and ladderback crack and break off. But one chair is not enough, so he gets the rest, all eight of them. He throws them all down, one by one, so that at the bottom of the stairs there's a dining room set left to us when my father's parents died, in a broken pile. Because of the garbage citations we've received, we can't even throw the chairs out into the street, and instead me and my sisters have to carry the broken chairs back up to the house and add them to the pile of garbage. The broken chairs sit high up there at different levels looking like any moment they'll tip over and block the path again.

John is fast-flipping his bin lids, adding the onions and sauerkraut and relish. Everyone wants a hot dog today. I sit on the curb and listen to the bin lids opening and closing and it reminds me of the sound the quarters, dimes and nickels make when you pay your fare and put them in the coin sorter on the city bus. I could sleep by that sound.

That night there is the feast and a ferris wheel to ride and I go up with Rena and her mother, who Rena never calls "Mom" but always "Bonnie," which is her real name, and Bonnie says there's nothing to be afraid of, and that I should look at the stars above the city and see how beautiful it is. At the top, when we're stopped for people down below to get off, Bonnie pulls out a black beauty from her change purse and pops it in her mouth and throws back her head to get the pill down. Her throwing back her head sets our car swinging and I tell her to please, please stop the swinging, but there's nothing she can do and so I crawl out from under the safety bar and Rena and Bonnie try to pull me back down and ask me, "Baby, where do you think you are going?" and now the car is really swinging and I don't know where I think I am going.

I look over the edge, I could shimmy down the ferris wheel bars with all the light bulbs attached and get back down to the ground where it's safe, where the zeppoli vats filled with hot grease cook dough, and people on church steps sit eating pizza and gyros. I could go down there and be with them, but instead I am standing up in the ferris wheel car and the man down below wearing one heavy-duty work glove and pulling the ferris wheel lever is yelling at me to sit the fuck back down and then people on all the other cars are yelling at me to sit back down and Rena and Bonnie are pulling me down by my arms until I am down on the dirty metal floor of the car by Rena and Bonnie's sandaled feet. I see that the silver polish Bonnie used to paint her toenails contains sparkles and they really are beautiful and look like millions of stars, more than I've ever seen in a city night sky.

I grow one tit first. My mother thinks it might be a cyst so she takes me to the free clinic where there are no private rooms, and in front of all the sniveling, runny-nosed poor children a doctor unzips my pants and pulls down my panties to check if the hairs of puberty have started to grow, which they haven't. So the doctor's miffed and tells my mother we should keep an eye on my tit, and for me to come back if the other tit doesn't start to sprout soon.

Rena's already got tits bigger than handballs. Boys at the beach come up to us and stand tall, shading our sun, and stare down at her tits, making comments, telling her she is fine, so fine. We talk as if the boys aren't there and then we go jump in the ocean and curl up and hold onto our ankles and feel the roll of the waves breaking over us. We stay like that for what could be hours, just lifting our heads up occasionally to breathe, and then returning back under the water. When we go to sleep at night we feel like we're still being rocked and swayed by the waves.

My father's slut is flat. Her bra size is A ad infinitum. My one tit is already bigger than either one of hers. She looks like an old mother monkey in the wild who breast-fed for years and now she's all dried up and all that protrudes are her two monstrous nipples that look like they've slipped halfway down to her belly. I know because my father has pictures of his slut nude framed around their apartment. I think my father loves her because she is so flat, because she's narrow at the hips and looks like a boy from behind with her short blond hair, and then she turns around and you realize from her face that she's a woman, and it's a surprise and I bet that's why he loves her.

We are the five little tomatoes and how they rotted in the heat of their loft, their mother mashed peel and seed sitting in her chair naked, smoking, watching Sunday war movies, Iwo Jima, *The Bridge on the River Kwai,* and the only breeze in the whole house is from me saying, "Kwai, Kwai, Kwai," over and over again because it makes a breeze come out of my mouth when I say it and I think me saying it is keeping me cool. The cats lie panting, their pink little tongues out and their eyes closed to near-slits. The sun beats down through the skylight in a large slanted rectangle, fading the cheap masonite boards that form our warped floor. We don't pass through that rectangle for fear we'll collapse from the heat so we sideline it on our way to the bathroom and there we blast the cold water from the shower and jump in and jump out and still dripping wet and naked we go back to our chairs and watch the ropy jungle neck sweaty tin canteen war world of the tropics on TV.

"What's that?" my mother says. It's just us, just our sweat collecting at the backs of our knees and dripping in a tapping rhythm to the ground.

17

"I thought it was code," my mother says. "I thought someone was trying to send me a message."

During the weekdays we've got Jesús who runs the freight elevator for the businesses on the floors beneath our loft. The Ouija board said it was he who stole my mother's ruby ring with the diamonds all around it, but my mother doesn't believe it.

"Merde, not Jesús," she says.

On our birthdays Jesús sings us "Feliz Cumpleaños" while we ride down in the elevator. He even gets Jochen, our German artist neighbor who rides down with us, to say "Happy Birthday" in German. "Alles Gute zum Geburtstag!" he says in a throaty loud voice that doesn't sound happy at all, but more like he's with the Third Reich, commanding us to march in a line and head for the showers. Then Jesús hands out a birthday present, a package of Funny Bones we eat on the way to school. But on Friday afternoons Jesús takes out his teeth and drinks rum and he does not hear the buzzer on the elevator and he does not come down and we pry apart the elevator door to make a crack so we can yell up the shaft, "Jesús, Jesús, Jesús!" Sometimes we have to walk up the steep five flights of dark stairs because Jesús never hears us.

John will not change. He says it's his corner and the other hot dog men can go to hell. They all want him to change and rotate and take turns at a different corner each day. He says his corner is the best corner and they all know it, but he was here long before they were, long before they even knew what a hot dog was, while they were still in their goddamn countries sucking at their mother's tits.

"I own this corner," he says to me. I think John is losing more teeth.

"Are you losing more teeth?" I ask.

"Yeah," he says and he sits down next to me on the curb because he can and because it's early morning and not lunch time yet. He puts his arm around me and lets his fingers come down and feel my tit and my nipple gets hard and I stand up and say, "John, how about a Hershey?" and he gets me one from where he keeps his spongy buns and I walk off and turn around saying so long and go into the park, but there is no one in it, only people passing through it taking shortcuts to work. There are no musicians playing music or pushers around whispering "tooeys, tooeys" in my ear.

When I pass by my sister Jody's room on my way to the bathroom in the middle of the night I can hear her pet mice squeaking and scuttling in their shavings and my sister snoring and our dog sleeping on the end of her bed, whining, her long dog nails scraping at the wall as she moves her legs and tries to run in her sleep. Maybe she's dreaming of saving one of us from a burning building or from where we lay frozen under snow from an avalanche.

Fuck, what a dog! I stop on my way back from the bathroom in the middle of the night and go into my sister's room and hug the dog while my sister still snores and the mice still scuttle and the dog wakes and licks my face and noses my ears and I go back to bed with her saliva on my cheeks, wiping it off with my rosebud pajama sleeve.

"What are the chances of that?" my father says, showing me a handful of change he took out of his pocket the other night onto his mantel and a quarter stood up perfectly balanced on the other coins without falling over.

"I don't know," I say.

"A billion to one?" he says.

"I don't know," I say.

"Amazing," my father says and says he won't touch the coin pile now. He asks how long I think that quarter will stay up there if he doesn't take it down or his slut doesn't take it down and I tell him I don't know. And I'm thinking it's a lot of change and if it doesn't fall down, I'll take it down myself and tell him it fell on its own.

One day I walk to the A & P and it's torn down and in its place is the E & B. Who's ever heard of the E & B? Polly and Tom are gone and I wonder where they went, what happens to grocery store saints? The E & B is filled with young workers, but Polly and Tom are old, who will hire them now?

I miss the loose-wired buzzer that would shock me when I rang for the butcher in the meat department to come out so I could tell him I wanted a meatloaf mix. There's no buzzer or butcher at the E & B, everything is already out in the cases, the parsley sprigs smashed under the plastic wrap that covers the already prepared meatloaf mix. I miss the discount at the checkout line I would get from Polly or Tom. I miss the stale fucking chocolate bunny rabbit handouts.

The phone rings and it's our grandmother and in French she starts talking to me even though I don't speak French and I tell her, "I don't speak French," but she keeps talking anyway. But it's not to me that she's talking, it's to her dog, Bambi, and I think in French she's asking Bambi if he wants another cookie, but I'm not sure. I hand the phone to my mother and I say, "It's Ma Mère," and my mother shakes her head and waves her hands and stomps her feet and mouths, "no, no, no" because she doesn't want to take the phone call, but I drop the phone in my mother's lap and my mother glares at me and then picks up the phone and says, "Cherie?"

Ma Mère comes over for dinner and gets so drunk my brother has to carry her down the stairs and call a cab and send her back to her hotel uptown by the park where she lives. While they're waiting for the cab, my brother's got to hold her from behind, his arms wrapped around her chest like she's choking and he's saving her life.

My sisters and I visit her uptown where she takes us to the Puffing Billy and we eat steak and she puts it on her tab and looks at my chest and tells me I'm turning into Gina Lollobrigida and then she tells my sisters they're fat and how did they get so fat and she will pay them a dollar for every kilo they lose. We say we don't know kilos, and then she says a dollar for every pound and my sisters say they'd rather be buried in a piano than be bought into losing weight. I point out the spots on her hands and tell her they're so brown, almost black, and I ask her if she's part black, part negress, and she shudders and tells me she is no such thing.

Jody tells her our brother is dating a black woman and she says no he's not, and we say yes he is and her name is Toffee and she says no it's not, you are lying to me, you are always making fun of me, but we tell her this time it's true, how we've all met Toffee and we like her, and we tell her the story Toffee told us of the time she was taking out the garbage in her apartment building and she opened the door to the incinerator chute and instead of throwing out her bag of garbage, she threw out her pocketbook by mistake, with everything in it, including her house keys and she had nowhere to go and how she walked down the streets, still holding onto the garbage, hugging it.

Ma Mère asks us how our father is and we tell her we don't see him much and she says we should, he's our father after all. She doesn't listen when we tell her it's not our fault we don't see him much and instead she tells us he was a good father. She tells us how when we were babies he was always unfastening our diapers our mother had just fastened because he thought she put them on too tight and he was afraid we could barely breathe or that our blood couldn't flow.

"I remember a trip to Central Park," she says. "He let you all ride the carousel, but he wanted to ride too, all of you together, so he chose one horse to ride, and the rest of you, you all rode on top of him. I don't know how he did it. One of you was sitting on his shoulders, the other hanging off his back, another seated behind him and one in front. The ticket taker didn't want to let him do it, but your father insisted it would work. He promised nothing would happen to you all and nothing did happen. Other fathers were looking at him that day. They were probably wishing they themselves could have been fathers as good as yours. Your mother shouldn't have left him," she says.

"He left her," we say.

After dinner we go upstairs and take her to her room that's just big enough for a bed and a table and a dresser with her liquor bottles on it. Bambi runs in circles when he sees us and then he starts to hump our legs and we kick him off and our grandmother says he's just saying hello and she gives him roast beef she ordered for him especially at the restaurant and adds ice to his water bowl. There's no closet in her small hotel room and when I use her bathroom the shower rod is hung with all her clothes and shriveled nylon stockings whose heels are black with dirt that won't wash out after having been worn so many times.

"Let's go," I say to my sisters when I come out of the bathroom, and we leave. She's already so drunk that she is talking to all of us in French, and we don't know French and she is showing us a book, the only book in her room, and she is saying something in French about the book and we look at the book and I expect a book in French, but it's *To Kill a Mockingbird* and she clasps it to her chest and smiles and lies back on her bed and closes her eyes.

We take the bus downtown and we're the only ones on the bus for the first few blocks and me and my sisters lean back in our seats in the brightly lit bus and listen to the peaceful sound of our coins in the change sorter clanging and going down as we head back to our house.

Our father has grown corn. It stands in angled rows to the midday sun. His garden is small, but he walks through it as if it were a field, taking long strides, letting silk cling to his sweater sleeves, pulling down ears, shucking them and biting into them raw. When he comes to the end of the row he turns around again and walks back through. He holds empty glasses up to the sun, saying he is looking at colors that are aqua and green and violet like his mother's eyes. He goes back to work on the Steenbeck and the image on the screen is of a soldier jumping over a log and then he rewinds and the soldier is jumping backward over the log and then forward again and then finally my father freezes the image of the soldier over the log in midair.

"That's me," our father says, "They needed a soldier in the film. I had boots and I bought fatigues. How about it? Would you know your father's leg?"

Later I walk outside calling for the cat. I can see my father's slut in their bedroom. She has come from the shower and there's a towel in a turban on her head. With arms crossed she looks out the window and I wonder if she can see me out in the darkness where I am calling for the cat. But she is not looking down, but looking up maybe, some kind of fortune teller who can read futures in passing dark clouds.

The cat comes with a mouse hanging from her mouth. The head is all the way in her mouth and the hind part drags on the ground. The cat is purring loudly and the tail of the mouse still moves and switches back and forth. My father comes outside, swaying, almost missing a porch step and the wine in the glass he holds sloshes onto the grass. The cat runs up to him to show him her catch.

"What is it to be that mouse? To be up inside all that thrumming purr?" he says while he pets the cat on the head and she closes her eyes.

At my father's summer place we go for walks on the beach. My father talks to the fishermen early in the morning as they pull their nets up the sand and pick through their catch. They give us their strays. A flounder and dogfish, a sea robin my father says is so ugly he can't imagine wanting to eat it. The mornings are foggy and we can't see the waves, we can only hear them close by us as we walk back to our car with the fish my father holds by the gills. He throws them onto the backseat where they lie on the vinyl. An occasional flop here and there as we drive back to the house. The slut eats dry toast and coffee and reads the paper in the living room. Holding the fish again by the gills, my father brings them in to show her.

"Oh, God," she says.

Then I'm put on the train again, back to the city. The slut

decided I had already stayed too long. It's early in the morning when I get to Penn Station. I don't take the subway home, instead I go to see John. I sit on my suitcase by his hot dog cart.

"How was your deserted island?" he says. That's what he calls Long Island. I tell him about the cat who ate the mouse and the ugly fish, the sea robin the fishermen gave us. John sits on his milk crate and then he says come here and makes me sit on his lap and I feel his fingers going up to my tits again.

Maybe once John had blond hair but now it's gray. He maybe once had blue eyes, but now they're so bloodshot it's hard to tell they're blue at all. More people pour into the park as the day heats up. I tell John I'm going for a walk and I go into the park and the place hums with noise, the ticking of spokes on bikes whizzing by, the hum of blacks in conversation, saying, "ahh hmm, mmm hhm," the motor of the fountain spouting water. I know how the mouse feels. Up inside all that thrumming purr.

We hear our brother violent in his room, angry. Toffee wants to leave him. He is knocking over shelves and then taking his mattress off his bed. We hear him grunting with the effort. He is pushing his mattress through the open window, a window wide enough to fit the mattress through. We are taking turns standing on the ladder in the hallway looking over the wall of his room, which is not a full wall, just a partition that doesn't reach the ceiling. We see the last bit of the green-and-white-striped mattress fitting through the window and then we run to the hallway window, my head and my two sisters' heads and our mother's head side by side hanging out the window watching the mattress fall to the street where cars have to swerve, horns blowing and people pointing up at us. We step back from the window and our mother says let's go downstairs. Jesús is already there with the freight elevator, already knowing it was our floor the mattress came flying from.

"Don't ask," my mother says to Jesús as we get inside the elevator and Jesús says he will not ask and Jesús stares at the peeling paint chip concrete wall falling away from us as we descend.

In the street we are heroes. We move the mattress to the sidewalk and a few drivers backed up the whole block long cheer and clap. The mattress, though, is soiled with dog shit.

"Leave it here," our mother says, "some bum will sleep on it." But my sisters and I have already turned the dog shit side down facing the sidewalk and we have jumped on the mattress and are all three laying down on it with our clasped hands held behind our heads and our legs crossed at the ankles.

"The clouds are cloudy," Louisa says and we see what she means, the sky layered with gray clouds and white clouds and puffy ones and streaked ones all at the same time. We can see no blue.

"Merde," our mother says and she sits down at the edge of the mattress and pulls a cigarette from her breast pocket and lights it with her lighter and smokes. Our brother comes down to the street wearing a blue silk robe that has a Chinese dragon shooting gold thread out of its flaring nostrils. As he walks past us, the robe's lapels gape and his smooth chest is bared.

"That's from my father," my mother says as our brother walks past. "He had no hair there either, and his face never even needed a shave," she says. "It's all passed down."

The traffic starts to lighten on our street as rush hour quiets down and it gets darker. My mother says let's eat dinner outside. So she brings down the pot of chicken and rice she has made and our plates and our forks and we set the pot on the curb and she doles us out our portions.

When we're done we go back up to our place, bringing the plates and the pot and leaving the mattress, now stained with grease since we wiped our fingers on it.

"We've left our mark," our mother says and then we all say so long to the mattress and wish that the next person who sleeps on it has sweeter dreams than the last person.

Days later, the mattress is gone and in the paper we read that a couple was killed while making love on a mattress in the subway tracks. "The sound of the roaring train got my girl hot," the dying man confessed.

Louisa's cray-pas drawings on the water heater start to melt. The faces of the boys she likes at school no longer look like faces and could be candle wax drippings instead. Louisa says it's all right since she doesn't like those boys any longer and we ask her who she does like and she doesn't say and instead she goes to the roof and leans against the wall of the elevator shaft, the part with the gears we can see through the elevator's skylight. She sits there, her head bowed, splitting the ends of her long hair while the gears go round and round behind her. When she does talk she says, "Bring me my French horn," and so I run downstairs and come back up with her instrument that hits the staircase walls as I go up because it's heavy and big and I'm small. She clicks open the case and there it lays gleaming and she takes a seat over the edge of our tall building, her legs dangling down to the empty lot below, and she puts the French horn's bell over her wide leg and her hand up inside it and she starts to play.

It's Mozart or Beethoven or Vivaldi or Bach. I swear the skinny trees down below seem to straighten their trunks and reach taller to hear her or to be nearer and have her music fall down softly on their leaves. Occasionally my sister has to stop and pull out her valves and blow, draining her spit. Water that will surely help the trees below grow. Jody hears her from down in our place and Jody comes up with her oboe and stands beside Louisa and together they play and I think if there are snakes below in that empty skinny treed lot, they are now sure to rise, charmed. Aren't all the boys at school in love with my sisters? But then they stop playing and they put away their instruments and they are just my sisters again.

"Dad was a chemist," our father says. "My mother was a housewife. She baked so much that every time she sat in a chair there was a rise of flour dust off her skirts."

"That's lovely," me and my sisters say and then we say we have to go, we have to get back downtown to our mother who is naked because of the too hot heat, relaxing on her day off, sitting and watching war movies on TV and running back and forth for her cold shower, and where, Oh Daddy O, is the money we're supposed to bring back to her? And he digs. The cuticles of his large fingers peeling back as he searches in all his pockets. Saying, "hmm," saying "well," and then looking around the room at objects as if he will give us a vase instead and that will help buy the food and I imagine myself setting a vase down on the conveyor at the checkout counter at the E & B in order to pay for my meatloaf mix. And he goes to the mantel, where the miracle coin, the billion-to-one-odd coin still balances on top of all the other coins and he says, "I hate to do this," and he scoops up all the coins that are there and slides them into a paper bag, a Balducci's paper bag, and he holds it up by the handles and he says, "Here." Then, "Oh, I was going to throw this out, but who wants it?" and it's a dirty black wastepaper basket, the kind sold with a blotter pad desk set, but the blotter pad and pencil holder don't come included in my father's deal, just the dirty old wastepaper basket that I take, because I don't have one and this one's free.

"Merde," my mother says, holding up the paper bag of coins and reading the writing. "Balducci's, the fancy place," she says. We stack the coins into piles of their denomination and then roll them into paper rolls using our school paper, the kind with lines.

In the morning, as my mother leaves for work, she tells me to walk the dog and take a roll of coins and go buy myself breakfast, a muffin and a juice at the Greek diner next door. We have been going to this diner for years and they know me by name. I tie up the dog to the pole that supports the ripped awning outside and I go inside the diner and get my muffin and my juice and I pull out a roll of my father's pennies to pay and Niko, his hair greasy and his apron splattered with Yankee Bean soup, says they do not take pennies. He will not accept them. I tell Niko, "Fuck, money is money," and he still says no and then I start yelling at him and asking him what's the matter with my money and his brother Spyro walks over and stands by Niko and tells me to get out of their restaurant. I can feel everyone in the restaurant slowly lifting up their heads from their eggs to watch the scene. When I leave the restaurant I slam the glass door behind me and all the glass shatters and comes cascading down in big pieces shaped like crescent moons that break into bits when they hit the ground. I go to untie the dog from the pole and Niko and Spyro run out after me and are yelling that they are going to call the police and they try grabbing my arm but I have untied the dog by now and she is barking and lunging at them and trying to go for their throats and the hackles on her back are raised so high she looks like twice the dog and I have to use all my strength just to pull her next door and back into the hallway of our place where I ring and ring the elevator buzzer for Jesús to come down and get me and when he comes I start crying and I tell him what happened.

He tells me not to worry and he takes me back upstairs and I sit down in a chair and the dog comes over and she puts her head in my lap and licks my face and whines and then she puts her paws up on me and I hug her and feel her cold chain collar on my cheeks and her fur. The coat fluffed big from having had her hackles up is wonderful. Oh, fuck, what a dog.

The police come. They knock at the door and I know it's them because I hear the crackling voices coming from their radios. Jesús is with them and he has pleaded my case and told them I am just a little girl, a good little girl, and the cops take notes while I tell them what happened and Jesús keeps interrupting and telling the cops that Niko and Spyro had no right calling the cops on such a little girl and he keeps asking the cops if they agree and finally the cops ask Jesús if he could get inside his elevator and run it a little, go up and down a few times while they finish talking to me. It turns out the cops don't want to arrest me, they just want to make sure I pay Spyro and Niko back for the glass door.

At the end of the day, when my mother gets home, I tell her what happened and she walks over to the diner and talks to Niko and Spyro and sets up a payment plan of ten dollars each time from her paycheck to pay for the door. I ask her why she's not mad at me and she says why should she be, it was a good thing it wasn't her they wouldn't take the roll of pennies from, if it were she would have broken the door and smashed their goddamn windows and then set fire to the place.

Our mother's cut herself by using a bare foot to swipe with her toes under the washer thinking she's swiping out a piece of plastic but really it's a thick shard of glass.

"Hold still, Mom," we say. We try to stop the bleeding by tying an old T-shirt around her foot.

"Blood is something else," she says, noticing how clean the kitchen floor has become after she wiped it with the sponge. The rest of the day she spends trying to peel back the T-shirt and see how her cut is doing.

"Leave it alone," we say.

"This is nothing," she says, "this will heal." For dinner we have no chicken, just rice. "Imagine each forkful a different dish," she says, so we take turns calling out the fare.

"Roast beef au jus," Jody says and we take a bite and comment how wonderfully rare.

"Peking Duck," Louisa says and we all say, "Mmm, how good."

"Rice," I say when it comes my turn and my mother and sisters all look at me and groan. "All right, all right," I say,

"Camel meat tartare," I say and my sisters say yuck, they'd rather I keep it rice, but my mother says, "You know, that may not be bad, on a hot sandy day in a tent with the flaps flapping in a wind after a hard day's ride to nowhere and back, camel steak tartare may just hit the spot," she says and eats a mouthful of her rice.

A red line forms up her leg from her cut. "It's just blood poisoning," she says the next day. "It could be hours before it travels to my brain." We take her to the hospital but we don't have money for a taxi so we put her on Louisa's bicycle. My sisters walk beside her steering the handlebars and I walk behind, letting her know when her long shirttail is about to get caught up in the spokes. "I could die like Isadora Duncan did," she says as we go down 11th Street. After an emergency visit she comes out with a shot in the rear and a bottleful of antibiotics. "Or I could just die swallowing all of these at once," she says and shakes the bottle like maracas.

Back in the house she throws an empty egg carton out the window that faces the lot, saying she hates to see the garbage pile up inside so fast. Then she takes her cigarette, which is burning on top of the refrigerator, burning black into the white, and she inhales and puts it back up on the refrigerator and opens the refrigerator door and claps her hands in front of it and says, "All right, what shall we have for dinner tonight?" She says, "Don't I get three wishes? Oh, wise and venerable Frigidaire, produce for my family a rack of lamb. No, eh? Is that the way it's going to be then?" There is mayonnaise and a half lemon in the refrigerator. The lemon is old and starting to mold and shrivel.

For dinner we have lemon mayonnaise sauce over rice. While we eat my mother says not to worry, tomorrow she gets paid and we'll have steak and potatoes, and then she says merde and goddammit to hell and then she takes her plate and throws it across the house so that it flies over the bed and smashes against the wall and the rice falls onto our bed. "Fuck your fucking father," she then says and she cries and covers her face with her hands and we continue eating our rice, very slowly, very quietly. We are hungry.

All night I cannot sleep for the smell of lemon mayonnaise sauce on my bed sheets making me sick. I sit in the chair instead and try to curl up. Above me, in the cracks in the wood of the wall, I can hear our cockroaches moving, a soft ticking sound when they jump to the floor and scurry around. I fall asleep. In the middle of the night I wake up because my brother is carrying me back to my bed. He's still wearing his blue silk robe and it feels so silky against me I think I could slip out of his arms and I want to hold onto him but I don't reach out because I don't want him to know I'm awake. He lays me down next to my mother and pulls the sheet up to my neck and tucks the sides under the mattress. I wait for him to leave and shut the door to his room. The smell of the lemon mayonnaise is still making me sick and I struggle out of the tucked-in sheet and go back to my chair up against the wall with the cockroaches in between the wood and I sleep and I dream.

* * *

He's under the catalpa in a wind that blows the pods off. They hit him on the head and fall to the porch deck. He rubs his bald head and heads for the pool, for the long-handled sieve he sweeps through the water while his slut swims backstroke. Her hands alternately out of the water, the pinkies separated and crooked like a tea sipper holding the handle of a fine china cup. My father circles the pool, skimming off leaves and blades of grass. My sisters and I were told not to swim while she swims, so instead we go to the kitchen, eat cheese and crackers we were told not to eat before dinner, drink orange juice we were told not to drink after breakfast, eat sliced ham we were told is only for lunch.

We run through the house screaming. Our brother has come to visit our father too, and he is It. He is chasing us, the belt of his blue silk robe loosening and loosening as he comes closer and closer to our backs we arch to keep him from tagging us. We are red-faced and hot and running up and down stairs and our brother is growling, he is some kind of bear or bull, and then the robe comes loose and he is almost naked in the hall, his shoulders bared, the robe hardly on him. Our father's slut walks in from the pool just in time to see our brother with his robe flying open, exposing himself. She runs away, and we hear a splash. When we look out the window, we see she has pushed our father in the pool. He is still holding the long-handled sieve and his shirt is filling with water, ballooning up.

She does not eat dinner with us. Our father goes to the bottom of the stairs to her room, telling her to come down, telling her he has made steak and ratatouille. We eat without her. We steal food from each other's plates. I steal steak from Louisa and Jody steals from me and our brother steals from all of ours and our father yells for us to stop. He loads a plate with steak and ratatouille and goes up the stairs to his slut's room. We hear the plate crash and break and our father comes down with the pieces and some ratatouille on his head. He puts the broken plate on the table and takes bread and soaks up what ratatouille is still left on one of the broken pieces. My sisters and I walk over to him, pull slimy bits of onion and eggplant off the middle of his head.

Then it's our brother who goes up to see her. He takes with him nothing but a glass of wine. My sisters and I follow him. He shoos us back, but we follow anyway. He knocks on the door and tells her who it is. The door opens just a little bit, not wide enough for anything to fit through except maybe a band of light, so my brother pushes it open more and goes in and closes the door behind him. We tiptoe up to the door, we listen from the outside. At first there is nothing, only what sounds like the soft whispering sound of our brother's robe swishing as he moves like he's showing her some private dance. Then we hear someone swallow. It can't be her, it's so loud. It's our brother. He hasn't brought her the wine. He's drinking it himself. Then there's a smash. The glass hits the door right by where our ears are pressed against it, trying to listen. Then we hear her laugh, it's a laugh that starts off low and then gets high. She's still laughing when our brother leaves the room and he's laughing himself, and just missing with his bare feet the glass that lies in shards beside the door.

In the morning my brother takes the car and drives us to the beach. It's starting to rain and no one is there. The sand gets pocked by the drops.

"Let's go in," he says and takes off his robe and dives into the water. I stand by his crumpled robe, the dragon face up, attacking the rain with his breaths of silk fire. My brother waves me in, saying it's not cold.

He's right, it's not cold when I dive in and then come up and stand waist deep in water while he tells me about the transfer effect—the way water is warmer than air when it's cold because the water steals the air's warmth. The same way, he says, that when you get into a bed with someone already in it, someone who's already been under the covers a long time, then you steal their warmth.

Maybe the transfer effect works with things other than temperature, I think. Maybe me hanging out with John all the time will make me somehow lose my teeth. I will feel Rena's mother's drugs, her woozy, swirly world. I will dream my mother's dreams, take on her French, speak words I do not even know as I sleep next to her, an unwitting thief in the night.

"Help! Help!" my brother says.

He is drowning for us. He is jerking around, splashing, waving in the water. The clouds roll dark behind him. The rain falls hard. He is letting ocean in his mouth, he is spitting it out, he is hanging from our necks, clawing at our skin, a comedian come up from the depths.

We are screaming "Let go of us!" The lightning, can't he see, the need for shore. And if only the dog were here, to grab his skin between her white front teeth to bite down hard and tow him back, tow us all out, get us all in the car, windows up, wipers on. We are being scratched by our brother's nails, he is climbing up us, a victim gone wild. Lifeguards must first learn how to kick the victims off them, how to unstrangle themselves from the clutching arms. Before learning how to save the drowning man they must learn to save themselves.

We know this, my sisters and I. We kick him good. Great kangaroo double kicks with both legs underwater up against his hairless chest as we try to slip through his arms. He's got us all three. He gurgles and slowly submerges while we see our chance and break for shore. We run for the car but he's got the key on a string on his wrist. We look back to him, what was him in the water, now just surf. His blue silk robe a dark thing that could be anything, a small tidal pool, a fisherman's cut discarded net.

Suddenly he is behind us, alive, roaring, naked, holding up his monster arms, and we are screaming and the thunder cracks and we grab the key and we are in the car with the rain on the roof and we do not know if the car is on. Who can hear it through the belting rain?

"Is it on? Is it on?" we say and he is out the door again, running for the silk robe under a pea green sky. Yes, it's on, and he's back in the car with his robe and we are on the road, the

43

sound of the windshield wipers soothing, a towel being passed around rubbed on all the wet girls' hair, denied to our brother for the drowning scare he gave us.

A pack full of Puerto Ricans chase me down in the park and make me crash and steal my bike. There's nothing I can do except run after them yelling for the police, but the Puerto Ricans disappear quickly. I run to the cop on horseback and stand by his stallion's shoulder and tell him what happened and he says there's nothing he can do. I tell him sure there's something he can do, he's got a stallion, why doesn't he take the stallion and gallop off and find my bike, and the cop tells me not to get so smart and I tell him I'll ride his stallion if he can't, and I'll get my bike myself. The cop pulls on the reins and turns and the stallion walks off and I run after the stallion and now I am talking to the stallion, telling it to fucking find my bike, asking the stallion what kind of a stallion is he anyway and I'm crying too and everything in the park is now blurry, and the stallion looks like it's swimming in water and not walking, and then it turns around and looks at me and snorts and shakes its head and I think the stallion is telling me that yes, it will try to find my bike, it will look for my bike even if the cop on his back won't, he will go to the ends of the earth to find my bike.

Oh, what a stallion, I think and I have a little-girl dream of owning my own stallion and riding him every day across open fields in the country.

John pulls out a milk crate, the milk crate he usually keeps for himself to sit on when it is not lunchtime and he tells me to take a seat and to watch the hot dog stand and that he will go after those Puerto Ricans himself and I see him go, his apron strings flying out behind him as he walks off. While he's gone I lift the lids and look inside the metal bins at the floating hot dogs in their greasy water. Some guy comes by and wants one, but I put the bun in the palm of my hand without first putting a napkin there and the guy walks off disgusted while I'm putting the hot dog in the bun. I'm yelling for him to come back and I'm waving a napkin in the air, saying, "Here, here's your fucking napkin," but he won't turn around. When John comes he's saying he couldn't find the Puerto Ricans who stole my bike, but I see he's putting his apron back over his head and he probably didn't go looking for my bike at all, but probably just had to take a crap in the park's public bathroom.

I see potential hot dog men on the six o'clock news every night. They are being bombed or rioting in their own countries, throwing Molotov cocktails at buildings already crumbled from some skirmish from wars before. Their women scream and lay down on the ground rocking the dead and injured, their hair come undone from buns at the backs of their heads, their feet bare, twisted out at odd angles under them, their bony ankles surely hurting against rubble on a blown-up road.

Our father has a new film to make. A documentary about thoroughbred racetracks. He has been funded by grant-lending institutions, but the money's not as much as he thought it would be. He can roll the camera, but who will do the sound for free? His slut says, not me, so he asks Louisa. She's terribly shy and he yells at her to get in there, to hold the microphone close up to the trainers' and the jockeys' faces. He has seen the film before he has finished making it, how it will start with the early morning mist and the sound of the hooves as the horses breeze by the rail.

At the yearling sales the buttery fat horses are led on the straw-covered stage. The auctioneer is red-faced from yelling out the figures, from pounding his gavel. Handlers click and whistle low and long when their horses rise up, wanting to exit the stage.

At a house he's rented to be close to the racetrack, he unloads his film inside a black bag and changes out the canisters, his hands hidden in the black cloth and the cloth moving, looking like an animal was captured inside.

"That was good," he tells Louisa. He means the whole day, the footage of horses having their teeth floated and their hooves shod. The blacksmith with the brand iron filmed in an orange circle of sparks. Louisa is sitting on the couch, sewing more patches onto the crotch of her blue jeans.

"It was a day from God," he says. "Tomorrow, the next day, days after, who knows, maybe we will have nothing but shit. But today," he says and he lifts up the film he has transferred into a metal can and he kisses it.

His shoulder is sore from holding the camera. He walks stiffly, sometimes massaging his shoulder as he walks around the kitchen, preparing the dinner with Louisa and me.

During the day I hold equipment for them while they film. I have learned to bet. Two dollars here and two dollars there. Our father has told me how and has explained exactas and trifectas. I understand past performance and bloodline.

Grooms chop carrots into feed tubs, and farther on down the shed row black hot walkers can be heard singing about how they will walk and talk with Jesus one of these days. Our father films a race and asks Louisa and me to go near the rail and take sound of the horses' hooves galloping by. In front of us a horse breaks down. While the others continue galloping, this horse stumbles forward on its knees. There is blood coming out of its nose and it is breathing hard. We know they will come and take it to the blue room and give it an injection and put the horse down. It's called the blue room because it's really just four walls with no ceiling. What the horse sees before it dies is the blue of the sky. The jockey jumps off and puts his hand on the horse's sweaty neck as it tries to stand but keeps falling back down on its broken leg.

"Whoa, whoa, sorry girl," is what we hear the jockey has said on the tape we listen to back at the house. Our father plays the tape over and over again. "Sorry girl, whoa, whoa, sorry girl," Louisa and I hear at night while we try to sleep in our beds.

At home our mother's arm rises up in her sleep and stays there. Could she be waving at her minions? At a dance with a partner just about to take her hand? At the riviera in the water, waving at her mother and her father on the shore?

"Merde," she says in the dark. We are in the dark again. My brother has figured out that we can get electricity from the outlet on the exit light. We plug in an electric pot and slow-cook a chicken while we wait in the hallway in the dark for it to be done. Louisa sits on the window ledge. It is five long flights down but she sits there almost asleep, her head drooping to the left, out toward the sky, as if the sky were some stranger's shoulder to lean upon throughout a trip on a train. She says she sleeps better sitting on the window ledge than in bed. I sleep on cheap scratchy sheets patterned like graph paper. It hurts my eyes to look at them too long. My bare arms and legs spread out on the sheets in this hot weather like lines drawn from axis points. Our mother hates our sheets. She is afraid some hot morning she will stand up from bed and on her naked body will be the squares and lines of the sheets from the cheap material's dye having bled with our sweat.

My brother takes his expensive guitars and throws them around in his room and crashes them against tables and walls so that the necks break from the bodies. Jesús comes up in the elevator and says, "Qué pasa?" and we tell him it's Toffee again and Jesús tells my mother she should call the police and my mother tells Jesús, "But Jesús, that's my son," and Jesús nods his head and then he goes home to the South Bronx after patting my mother on the back.

Suddenly my brother opens his door and he runs into the closet and pulls out the twenty-two and the bullets and meanwhile my mother is pulling at his arm and screaming for him to put the gun away, but he doesn't and he just throws my mother against the bookshelf. Still holding the gun and the bullets he goes back into his room and slams the door. My mother is hurt at the bookshelf. She can't catch her breath and books fall down around her, their dusty covers dirtying her face and shoulders. The dog is barking, running from my brother's door to my mother.

"Shh," my mother says to the dog and lifts her finger to

her lips. We lift my mother up from the pile of books that have rained down around her and she goes to my brother's door and she calls to him and bangs on the door but he tells her he will shoot himself now if she doesn't go away, if she doesn't leave him alone. The only one he will talk to, he says, is our father.

The phone company in our neighborhood is on strike. No one has service except an emergency phone center set up a few blocks down in a hotel lobby. "Call your father," my mother says to me and Jody, "and run," she yells, so me and Jody run to the hotel and there's such a long line winding around the outside of the building that if we wait on it it could be too late.

"My brother's got a gun, he's going to kill himself, let me use the phone!" Jody starts to scream and the people make way and everyone is staring at us while Jody is fumbling for the dime and someone reaches out and gives us one and Jody calls our father where we know he's staying at his apartment uptown.

He comes down on his bicycle wearing a beret. The bicycle is a WWII bicycle, army green with a clever design that features a wing bolt in the center support bar that when loosened lets the rider fold the bicycle in two. The beret is black wool. He leaves it on when he stands on the top of a ladder outside my brother's door and tries to look down over the wall of my brother's room that doesn't reach all the way to the ceiling. The folded bicycle rests against the hallway wall looking deformed.

This night my brother doesn't kill himself and I finally

fall asleep with the image of my father still on the ladder with his beret on talking to my brother over his wall.

My mother's bruise on her arm from my brother throwing her against the bookshelf heals like a hurricane swirl seen on radar when the weather's reported on TV. The eye is the purplest part, the part that days afterward still makes her say merde after she brushes by accident up against a wall.

My brother stays inside all the time and lets his hair go greasy like the hot dog men. I come home and he is watching all the soap operas I've watched for years, asking me who the characters are, asking me to catch him up on years of destroyed lives.

He still keeps the gun in his room and sometimes I can hear him opening it and I don't know why, except I think to look into it, at all the black that he can see.

It's dark in Rena's basement where she's having a party and we play spin the bottle. Whenever the bottle spins to me I kick it with my toe so I won't have to be kissed because I know the boys all want to kiss Rena instead. I leave them in the basement and go upstairs. It's the middle of the day and Bonnie isn't home but Bonnie's Hells Angel boyfriend's motorcycle is parked in the middle of the floor and I see him sleeping on Rena's mother's bed. He sleeps naked. On his arms I see tattoos so faded I can't tell what they are. I walk up close to him. He needs to shave and in the corners of his mouth is white spittle. He smells like some kind of liquor he either drank or threw up. His eyes move back and forth under his veiny eyelids shiny with grease or sweat. His eyelashes have lint stuck to them. There's a round scar on his forehead that looks like a doctor didn't know where to give him a vaccine and stuck it in his forehead instead. He whines a little, like our dog does in her sleep. I watch his feet too, to see if they'll move the way her paws move, but they don't. They are like women's feet, pale and long and thin. Fuck, this Hells Angel would die in the desert, I think. He would die in the jungle, in the wilderness he would not survive. Bonnie walks in.

"Hi, sweetie," she says to me and takes off her clothes in front of me and then sits on her bed and swallows a pill from a bedside waterglass and lies down next to her Hells Angel and closes her eyes.

I walk home. It's hot and all the gum stuck to the street once dried has now gone to goo again and collects on the bottoms of my shoes and when I walk it's like moonwalk, a slow labored lift for each foot, the gum in strings I try to walk off. I stop at a phone booth and check the change return for coins. I find dimes and nickels and then I turn to go, but I decide to put the coins in the slot and start dialing my father. His slut answers and says he's not there. I want to know where he is but she says goodbye and then hangs up on me before I get the question asked.

The telephone booth floor is metal and rough, a good floor for wiping off the bottoms of my shoes, which I do, saying at the same time, "That fucking slut."

A woman wants to use the phone, she raps on my glass

door with a coin. I don't look at her. I keep wiping off my feet. She starts pressing her face up against the crack in the door, telling me I'm not using the phone, so I should let someone else use it.

"I'm using it," I tell her and then I lift my foot up as high as it can go and I pull the phone off the hook and I start using the mouthpiece to wipe the gum off the bottom of my shoe.

At home the telephone rings, but we can't find it. We find the cord, hold it with both hands and crawl and follow it like bomb specialists in search. It's deep under our tower of garbage.

"Let the damn thing ring itself to death," our mother says. But couldn't it be some boy? Some cray-pas boy drawn to the best of Louisa's abilities? Or could it be our father?

"Oh, find the phone," we say. We stand up on all the bags and toss them down where they split and ooze black liquid, where their ties come undone and hellish stink rises up in vapors and so we open up our mouths to breathe through them instead. The ringing gets louder. Wipe the maggots off it, I yell to Jody, who has found it first, who instead of wiping them off, flicks them while they lift and curl hidden in the dial holes.

"Hello," Jody says. And it is our father and we sit down on the garbage and listen.

"What are we doing?" Jody says, she looks around her at the garbage everywhere, and then at me.

"Watching television," I say.

"Watching television," Jody says into the phone.

"Let me talk now," I say and Jody turns away from me so I can't grab the phone. Finally it's my turn, and there is nothing much to say and I can hear him wanting to get off, playing with something in the background, my sister talked him out and now he is talkless and bored. I hear something in the background. More coins on his mantel? The clasp on a briefcase? And then I know, I figure it out, it's the hinge on his refrigerator, opening and closing. He is perusing for a meal.

"When can we see you, when can we visit?" I say. He is busy, oh so busy, there is the film, its early-morning and every-day hours.

"Do you know," he says, "that some people don't know the sun is a star? Do you know?"

He says there are more morons than you can imagine, more stupidity in the world than we could ever think up, the statistics are astounding, the stupid rule the earth, never be smart, if you want to learn something, any one thing in your life, you must learn to never be smart because you will lose every time. "Learn to be stupid," he says. "It pays."

Then we ask him again. Can we come, please? we say and he says all right. We are allowed once again to visit him at his summer rental.

The corn is ready to eat. There are special instructions to follow. Instructions my father's father insisted on. Boil the water first, then go to the garden and pick the ears from the stalks and run with them in your arms to where the water is boiling on the stove. Shuck the ears as quickly as possible, as close as possible to the boiling water, let the husks fall to the floor, don't even spend time leaning over a trash pail trying to make sure the silk doesn't go all over the place. Cook the corn for no longer than four minutes. Use a timer. Don't cover the pot. Roll the corn back and forth on top of a stick of butter. Use hickory-smoked salt. Enjoy. When you are finished biting the kernels off roll the cobs in butter again, suck on them, then roll them again in the butter a third time and throw them outside where the dog can hold them between his front paws and gnaw on them for hours.

My father is ripping off the husks. Silk is hanging from his elbows and his forearms like tassels from a cowboy's suede coat. His slut is amused. She's sipping wine. Behind her in the window I can see the sun setting over the fields.

"Faster! Faster!" she says, she laughs and sips. The windows start to steam and I can no longer see out them. We eat with the cornsilk and husks still in a pile on the floor by the stove.

"You can smoke it," my father says and after dinner, while his dog is gnawing on his corn, my father rolls the silk in cigarette paper and lights it. It burns so quickly there's not even enough time to put your lips to it and inhale. His slut laughs.

"You'll smoke your fingers instead," she says while standing in the doorway. The stars are out. So many stars my father can't find the constellations. He's seeing handles of big and little dippers in groups of stars that are constellations not yet named.

* * *

One day our father comes to our house.

"What's he want?" our mother says, looking out from the window, watching him jump off his bicycle and come through our doors. He wants things that belonged to his parents, he says. Things he says that are rightfully his. He heads first for an Indian bowl.

"The Navajos used it to cook," he says. There are fire stains going up around the sides. The old bowl, passed on down from his great-grandparents, is worth money, he says, and he will have it appraised. Our mother seethes. She holds her hands in fists jammed into front pockets of her cardigan. We can see the bumps of knuckles plainly through the wool.

Our father takes the bowl off our shelf.

"Leave it," she tells our father.

"Oh, no. This is mine," our father says. "This was never yours."

"I want the money from it, then. Money for the children," our mother says.

"Sell it? Sell it?" our father says. "You don't know anything. You don't sell something like this. That's what a dumbshit would do. That's what an asshole would do."

Our mother runs up to our father, her fists coming out from her cardigan pockets.

She flies at our father's back, her hands still fists, a bit of lint from her cardigan pocket perched on a white knobby knuckle.

And then she rides him, her legs wrapped around his waist while she hits him all over—at his head, into his eyes and then he starts to yell that she's blinding him, and "Ahhh," he yells, and "Ow" and our mother still hits him and I wish the dog were here, because if she were she would bark and bite at either of them and somehow make them stop, but the dog is out with Jody and it's just me and Louisa and Louisa isn't doing anything, she's just watching, and so I go and I pull our mother off our father's back. I grab her hair and pull it with all my weight. She lets go of our father and falls to the floor and she's hurt, grabbing a bruised elbow and crying with her eyes closed.

Our father is leaving now with the bowl under his arm. He is walking backwards out the door, maybe not wanting to leave his back exposed to her. When I was very small I would tiptoe to the edge of their bed, his face close to hers, and wonder if they were dreaming the same dream. Then he would roll over, or she would cough, and I would walk backwards, the way he is doing now, only tiptoeing. I left because I didn't want to wake them. I didn't want them to stop having the same dream.

In his bicycle basket on his handlebars he keeps a hammer for banging on trunks of taxis that cut him off as he rides. He has learned how to weave through the traffic and run the red lights when the taxis realize what happened and start chasing after him. He wears rubberbands around one ankle, to keep the flare of his pants from getting caught in the chain. When he is tired he holds onto the bumpers of buses to catch a faster ride. Is his slut in the kitchen when he comes home? She is snipping parsley with scissors, neat little cuts whose repetitive sounds are pleasant to his ear. He stands behind her, wanting to encircle her waist, but she turns to face him, the scissors' tips held close to his neck still stuck with leaves from the parsley. "Oh, Jesus," he says. He moves away her hand holding the scissors.

"Snapper," she says, pointing to the broiler that's on with the tips of the scissors.

He moves to the living room, sits in a chair. He touches the skin around his eyes and then closes them, lightly touching the lids.

"All the ride uptown I saw stars," he says.

"Lemon?" she asks, her hand held over the snapper she's pulled from the broiler and put onto plates, ready to squeeze a lemon wedge.

"Tea bags, won't that bring the swelling down?" he says. She squeezes the lemon anyway over his fish.

After they've eaten, he lies on their bed, his hands resting on his chest, his thumbs hooked under his armpits and he looks at the ceiling.

"Christ almighty," he says.

His slut takes the keys off the mantel, says she's going out for a walk.

"It's turning cold," he says, before she closes the door.

Summer's at an end now. At night a hurricane hits and the wind is so strong it ripples the skylight glass. We watch from our beds, not able to hear each other talk because the sound is so loud. We play hurricane roulette and try to see who can run to the bathroom and back before the next flash of lightning. I run and I trip and fall and lose and the whole house and all of us in it are lit up white by the lightning and I see my sisters laughing at me with their heads thrown back in their beds, their mouths wide open, the ridged roofs white like ribs, like carcasses standing in sand bleached by sun.

Our mother's neck is falling. She firms it with slaps. One after another right under her chin.

"Merde, in France, well you know, in France, never, never this," she says.

She is chapped at the ear tips. Hung skin on her lips, raspy at the elbows, and low in the mouth when she yells "Count me in" across the house. We are up all night with Atlantic Avenue and Park Place and the lost silver car and terrier dog replaced with bottle caps and garbage twist ties fashioned into lumps that won't blow off the board. Cheating is rampant. Hands passing hidden orange 500s under the tabletop and stolen hotels plunked on property never fully paid for. The game is not the game, but the cheating of it all. We play until night bleeds out dawn, until our mother's eyeliner has crusted and balled in her tear ducts she's so tired. "Good morning," we say and go to sleep. Our brother is sponging his robe, wiping out spots from sipping hot chocolate whose froth slid and soaked the dragon's scaly tail. "Water stains too," we tell him from under our covers deep in our beds.

"Really?" he says. "Oh, fuck, fuck, fuck," he says. "Why didn't you tell me?" he wants to know. He comes at us with water, throwing it on us from a bowl left in the sink. The bowl once had something in it like milk, held curdled bits in its curved sides that now lace through our hair like unmelting snow from some Hollywood holiday set.

In the morning kids in front of school are burning required reading in a bonfire right in the middle of the street. I see *Catcher in the Rye* go up in flames. I would go grab it, but they're all the cool kids who smoke and cut Hygiene and still get good grades, so I don't go near them. They are smarter than I am and have vision and reasons for doing things I may never understand. If Vietnam were now they'd protest it and I'd probably think the fucking Communists should be shot down. I'd find reasons to agree with our government because it would be easier. I don't want to be hit with a club and tear-gassed and trucked off to jail.

After school I go over to Rena's and Hells Angels are riding their motorcycles through her loft. Bonnie's boyfriend cuts hair in a salon and after work he brings his friends over to Rena's and they do drugs at the long kitchen counter sitting on stools and then move back to their bikes, gunning their engines, turning fast turns on one back wheel that burns rubber and smokes up the air.

Rena's got a beagle named Muy Hombre and he walks himself around the neighborhood and when he comes back he scratches at the downstairs door so that we let him in. Often he comes back with dirty fur as if he'd been crawling through tunnels but Rena says it's from the bums on his route who all know his name and call to him and pet him with their filthy hands.

Rena's building is three lofts all connected by trap doors. She lives in the bottom, her grandfather lives in the middle, and her aunt on the top. We go through the trap doors and visit them and leave the Hells Angels behind. We open the trap door and go up the ladder and we hear Mozart on her grandfather's stereo and he's painting with oils on a canvas. Rena says not to talk to him while he's painting so we just pet his Persian named Monet and then head up to her aunt's. She's got crystals in her windows and a pet skunk named Toro who lives under the couch. Toro's scent glands were cut out, but not all the way, and so the place still smells like skunk, but we hardly see Toro and only hear him at night with the lights off when he runs back and forth in the loft for what Rena's aunt calls his midnight stroll.

We sleep at Rena's aunt's loft because Bonnie and her boyfriend and the rest of the Hells Angels are still zooming around Rena's loft on their bikes. In the night I wake up to Toro nestling and rooting in my hair and I pick him up and throw him across the room but he just comes back and at school all the next day I stink like skunk and I just want to go home and wash.

It's blood day and during Wood I see out the room's windows and into the windows of the nurse's office where the tough lesbian gym teacher, Miss Tord, who we call Miss Turd, is about to give blood. When the nurse sticks in the needle, Miss Turd faints and I yell and point to show all the other kids, and the sawing and hammering stops and we're all laughing and watching the nurse slapping Miss Turd's face. Mr. Lenin, who's got a forest of black hair up his nostrils, comes over to tell us to get back to our projects, but when he sees Miss Turd facedown on the nurse's desk, he says, "Oh, eet's Miss Turd," and watches too while he picks at his nose.

I'm making a box, but Mr. Lenin has to do everything for me because I don't like holding the wood and pushing it through so close to the blade of the circular saw. Mr. Lenin tells me I have to sand and glue, but I don't do that well either and when you pull out the drawer to the box the sides are slanted like a parallelogram and not a rectangle.

"You must do it again," Mr. Lenin says, but I say I won't

and he says I'll fail and I say I don't care and I don't know what good is a box if I have nothing to put in it and he tells me I can put a paper and a pens in it and I tell him I don't need a place for a paper and a pens and Mr. Lenin walks away from me and I think it's because of the stink of Toro in my hair.

"Merde," my mother says when she gets back from work that night, "lucky none of you were on that boat," she says, speaking of a ferry where a man plunged a samurai sword into passengers' bellies. She always thinks we are where a disaster is, even plane crashes when none of us have ever flown. On our street a bus once caught the legs of an old woman and rolled over her skull. My mother was convinced it was one of us and up above from our window my sisters and I could see our mother pushing her way through the crowd, hitting at onlookers' shoulders to make room for her so she could get down low and see.

There's no money for the rent so we sell the piano for less than half its worth. Later that night we miss the cats walking across the keys, waking us up to sometimes a lighthearted tink-tinking and other times a low and sinister roll from the darker range.

"Not my parents' piano!" my father yells the next day when he comes over to collect more of his things and then he yells "Jesus Christ" in front of the space where the piano used to be.

Now there is floorboard that is shiny and looks new because it's never been stepped on. I wonder if he can see himself yelling in the reflection of the shiny board, the way I can see him. His face is turning purple and the spots on his head are white compared to the rest. There's a bulging vein in his neck that makes me stand back from him and go out the door for fear I'll get sprayed when it bursts with a jet of his hundred-proof blood.

Jody lets her mice climb her head and shoulders and holds out her arms so the mice can climb out to the ends of her fingers. She closes her eyes and smiles.

"They tickle," she says. "Want to try?"

"Fuck no, get those mice away," I say.

She hums when she cleans their cage. She tosses the dirty wood shavings out the window.

"For the wild mice," she says. She coughs while she cleans, sending up the shavings from their cage.

"You'll infect them," Louisa says. "They'll die. You've given them mouse bronchitis, all right in humans but deadly in mice."

The phone rings. It's Ma Mère, very drunk. She's talking French to us, but our mother is not around to pass the phone to.

"We don't understand French," we say and we hang up the phone. She calls back again, this time we yell it, "We don't understand French!" and then we slam the phone down. When the phone rings a third time we don't bother even saying hello, we just start yelling, "We don't understand French."

We're not sure if our brother's stopped trying to kill himself. He still wears his blue silk robe opened at the chest all day long. He still goes out at night with his guitars and comes back late. My mother still clears a path for him and it seems as if she takes longer to do it now. Pushing all the chairs to the farthest they can go against the walls, even sweeping now as if afraid he might trip on a hairball and that might send him off running to get the gun and aim it at his head.

He wears his Chinese blue silk dragon robe to the deli next door. He buys a bran muffin and hot coffee that he pours from the self-serve counter and drinks while standing there and then fills up his cup again.

"Kung fu, grasshopper?" the deli man says and then holds out my brother's nickel change in the palm of his hand. My brother doesn't grab the coin from the deli man's hand, instead he pops a fist up under the back of the guy's hand and the nickel flies up and my brother catches his change.

Jesús isn't around so we have to walk up five flights of stairs. At each landing my brother stops and drinks more coffee and bites into his muffin. At the last landing he sits down and says he thinks he'll finish it there. He asks me if I think someone threw me down all those flights of stairs would I die or would I just be crippled and have to have my piss and shit collect in some plastic bag.

Upstairs our mother says, "Merde, all of you get out of this goddamned house," and she asks for her purse and we get it for her and she opens her wallet, but there's no money in there, so she digs at the bottom of her purse for coins and then empties her purse onto the floor. Little bits of tobacco from broken cigarettes float through the air. She sifts through it and finds some silver and she asks for our hands and she puts it in our palms, along with the bits of tobacco stuck to the coins. She waves us away and tells us to go buy ice cream in the park and to go play and have some fun. But we don't leave. We've got work to do. Her artist friends have arrived. They've volunteered their driving and their cars and they line their cars with plastic drop cloths already splattered with dried paint. In the cars, we push our garbage bags far back into the ledges by the rear windows, so that from the outside the garbage looks so uncomfortable crammed up against the glass, and all the tops of the bags cinched with red ties look like puckered mouths pressed there and when the cars drive off me and my sisters feel the need to wave, saying so long to months of tuna cans we ate out of and milk cartons we drank from, months of cat litter we scooped, months of brittle ends trimmed from our long hair, months of nail clippings, months of overdue notices from the library, cut-off notices from the gas and electric, late notices and skip notices from school we never showed our mother, rotten things too, the potatoes sprouting white gnarled roots, the green mold curd in a cottage cheese container, mouse-bitten bread wrappers, the doodles done while talking on the phone, the phone itself, slammed too many times on Ma Mère, on our father, the blue, yellow, and red wires piggy-tail curled sticking out from the unscrewed mouthpiece as if all the exclamations and curses screamed over the line had broken the phone and snapped the wires.

I go to see John who is low on hot dogs and he sends me to Gristede's with ten dollars to buy some Hebrew Nationals. He says he hates doing it, the damn taste is not the same as Sabrett, and then he spends the afternoon watching the other hot dog men with binoculars, seeing how their business is doing compared to his own. John lifts me up and sets me on the light change box and perched there I watch the park. It's a day when everything is clear and clean, there was a rain the night before and now the metal bench arms glisten and the leaves on the trees are bright green and the jungle gym bars shine and look cool to the touch. My horse, my stallion, has his head held high. His mane, lighter brown than his hide, seems to ripple like water going over a fall as he walks on the paths. "Look at me. Look at me," I command silently in my head to the stallion, but he doesn't look at me and the cop who rides him turns him around back through the crowd.

* * *

Outside police car sirens are wailing.

"They're coming for us, or just for me," our mother tells us at home. She holds out her arms and crosses them at the wrists and closes her eyes. "Take me," she says, "it's got to be better than here."

"Take us too," we say, and cross our wrists the way she does, waiting for the cuffs that never come. Then the siren sounds slowly fade. That night there's a thunderstorm whose lightning bolts have come to pierce our skylight glass. We're sure of it. We huddle by our mother.

"You're afraid of this? Oh, please," she says.

Jody wants to call Dad.

"I'm sure he's more afraid of this storm than you are. Go ahead, call him if you want to." We don't. The lights have gone off and all we can see is the lit end of our mother's cigarette burning brighter when she inhales. It's such a relief, the glowing red light and the sound of her breathing in and breathing out and the deep rattle we can hear within her, percolating at the bottom of her lungs.

Rena goes to Greece and sends me postcards of the Acropolis with a big arrow she has drawn behind a pillar. She writes this is where she kissed a boy. Then there is another arrow and she writes this is where Bonnie kissed a man. She phonetically writes out a Greek curse for me and I use it on my sisters and when I walk by the diner whose glass door I smashed. I use it on John to see if he knows it but he's not listening, he's busy cleaning the hot dog cart, dipping his apron corner into the hot hot dog water and then running the apron over the metal, over the handles, over the umbrella frill that's dirty with grime, over the pole and the spokes on the wheels and the handle he pushes every morning when he comes to the park and every evening when he goes home.

I grow the other tit. It too starts like a cyst, hard, and it moves like a quarter back and forth under my skin. My mother makes fun of my tits. She grabs at them and pinches them when I undress. "Bee-boop" she says when she pinches one and then

71

the other. I hit her hands and slap them hard and push her away. I start to dress where she can't see me, leaning over the radiator to hide myself when it's cold, or changing in the shower stall when it's not so cold. When I'm bored she tells me the French have a saying, she says I should go take my titties and dance. "That's your saying?" I say.

"That's it," she says.

"Tell me more," I say.

"I can't remember," she says.

"Yes, you can," I say.

"I was in love with my cousin. I would swim with my cousin in the ocean, naked of course, at night without moonlight. We would race to a buoy and then back. We swam so close side by side that sometimes we would touch. But it was dark, merde, who knew what we were touching. Something soft and fleshy, a body part we could hardly name. He was tall. My nose came right here," and she touches me right at the arch of my ribcage. "I could fit my nose in there. He said either his ribs were made from my nose or my nose was made from his ribs because they seemed to fit so perfectly. Merde, he was a poet. He said we fit together like the world before the world was continents before the world broke up and drifted apart."

"What about Dad, what do you remember?" I say.

She starts to cough. She coughs all the time. A cough that lasts through my dreams at night. She gags sometimes, she coughs so much. Her neck puffs up, her eyes bulge and tear. She takes a drink of her drink to keep her from coughing, but she still coughs. She cannot answer my question.

* * *

The landlord won't fix the windows. Gusts of winter wind blow through the broken glass fallen out from rotted wooden frames. Snow comes in at an angle, collecting on the floor. The cats step in it and lick their paws. My brother staples plastic to the inside of the windows. Lights from cars and street lamps are just blurs. The snow collects on the skylight. We wake up and we can't see the sky. It's quiet, as quiet as if we had slept in a cave.

"I hope the roof holds," my mother says.

We are cold at night. We sleep with sweaters on and hats. The cats claw at our faces, they want to get under the covers too. We let them in and keep our heads under the covers, breathing in what the cats breathe out.

There's a fire outside in the empty lot, but who would know except for the heat. It's a fire seen through plastic, the flames a blur of orange. We are told to evacuate. We take the cats in pillowcases and sit on the curb in the snow. The firemen ax down our downstairs door even though we keep telling them we have a key. My brother tries to buy a coat off one of the firemen, but the fireman won't sell. We say we would be better off inside, at least we wouldn't be cold, our building's brick warmed by the raging fire in the empty lot.

"What's this? What's this?" our mother says.

"Your hair," we say. It's coming out in clumps held between her fingers.

"My hair?" she says. "It never did this before," she says. "What's going on inside of me?" She bangs her fists on her head. "Your father did this to me," she says. "All those years," she says.

The firemen say it's safe to go back in. To fight the fire out back they've gone through our place. The floor's one huge puddle from their leaky hoses. They've pulled off all the plastic hanging, and now the wind is coming through again. The puddle freezes like a pond in our house and we take turns sliding across it wearing our coats and our gloves and our hats and the dog is with us on the ice, sliding too, barking, biting at our coattails and sleeves, trying to pull us away to the safety of shore.

We are smoked through. Our clothes in drawers, our mattresses, our furniture, it all smells like the fire did out back. We run the washing machine for days, one load after the other while the poor machine shakes and dances across the kitchen floor. What trees were out back are now just charred and when a wind comes along, cinder bits and ash fly into our window like black snow.

"A black Christmas," our mother says, holding out her hand to catch it. It is Christmas. We have a tree with no branches at the top, only a spindly long point, and a few fuller branches at the bottom. The cats eat the tinsel and we can hear them throwing up all night. Ma Mère comes over with a basket of fruit. She won't sit on our car seat couch unless we spread a towel there first. My mother pours her wine. "Joyeux Noël," we all say and then there is nothing to say and we walk away and leave my mother talking French to her until dinner. After dinner Ma Mère needs help to the bathroom. We take her in there and get her pants down and sit her on the toilet. She falls over and we pick her up again. There are tears running down her closed eyes.

"Quest-ce que tu fais?" our mother asks her.

"My girdle," she says in French to my mother and my mother tells us to help her unfasten Ma Mère's girdle. Once her girdle is off she slides forward, her head falling back and banging on the tank of the toilet seat, the gray sparse hair between her legs visible now, as her pubic bone is pushed out toward us. My mother props her up again.

"Pee-pee already!" my mother says to Ma Mère, but Ma Mère starts to laugh and says she cannot. "Oh, damn you, pee-pee!" my mother says again.

"Come on, pee-pee!" my sisters and I say. We are all laughing now, and kneeling on the floor of the bathroom, trying to hold Ma Mère up.

"Pee-pee!" my mother tries to say again, but she is laughing so hard she cannot say the word. Ma Mère starts to cry, great sobs that make her thin shoulders go up and down. Her nose runs and we wipe it for her.

"It's okay, ma cherie," my mother says to her and hugs Ma Mère and Ma Mère cries louder and grabs onto my mother and tries to stand but she cannot and so she is just sort of hanging off my mother, her pants down by her ankles and then she starts to pee. She pees all over my mother's legs and my mother's feet. "Oh, merde!" our mother says.

"No, c'est du pee-pee," Ma Mère says.

Our mother says, "C'est vrai, ce n'est pas de merde, c'est du pee-pee. Oh, damn you all," our mother says.

Our mother is fingering the crocheted holes in her shawl, poking her bright red painted nails through, wiggling them around. She is braiding the tasseled ends and furrowing her brow. She has noticed the lines. She has held up the hand mirror and mentioned how the windfall of money she hopes to someday be hit hard with will go straight to her brow, her crow's feet and a lift of her chin.

"We are fucking poor," she says. She looks for things she can sell. She digs out old bullfight posters from Spain with the names of famous matadors on them she was given as a wedding present from the cousin she was not supposed to love. "If I sell these I may well have never loved him and he never loved me," she says. "Or something like that." She rolls up the posters and puts them back in the storage room. "Merde," she says, "I'm going through my phases," and then she faints on the floor in the hallway. Jesús has to help us stand her up and get in the elevator and as we go down she keeps saying she's hot and then she asks us over and over again, "Aren't you hot? It's so hot. Am I the only one who's hot?"

That night she sweats next to me in bed, and I become hot too when I wasn't hot before, and I lay awake, thinking how it's a sign of the transfer effect taking place. In the morning she tilts her head back, dropping in drops to rid her eyes of red. The drops spill down her cheeks and I think for a second how the tears could be real.

Our mother lights her cigarette and keeps its ember end out on the edge of a dresser. The dresser drawer is stuck open and ashes fall and collect there, a high pile of them she has never thrown out.

"Save them. Spread them over oceans, over my homeland, over patisseries and boulangeries, when I die."

We leave for school and she is still not made up. Her bald spot not yet covered over by her teased surrounding hair, not yet drawn on and hidden by grease pencil. Her eyelashes not yet curled with the eyelash curler that is stuck with so many eyelashes lost to its clampy torturous design.

It starts to rain at the park and John tells me to stand with him under his hot dog umbrella. I stand in front of him, my belly warm up against the metal bins, while he stands behind me. Sandwiched like that I let him touch me because I'm hungry and a hot dog would taste good. Pressing up against me he tells me about his homeland.

"Go home," I tell John, and he says not to worry, the rain will stop soon and the hot dog eaters will reappear in the sunshine.

"No, go all the way home," I say. "See your children, see your wife." John steps back from me.

"Move," he says. "I've got to turn up the flame."

A man below us shows loud foreign films at night for two dollars a seat. Our mother pounds a pot on the floor to make him stop. The banging of the pot, she thinks, will make him turn down the volume. You'd think it would be worse when the films are talking, but what we can't stand is when they're silent, the music blaring and distorted and so dramatic we have dreams of falling down ravines and being chased by black-clothed men. When it's foreign it's no language we can say. Swedish or Kurd, Pakistani or Welsh, we have no idea. Our mother says we should all go down there in our beltless bathrobes and storm through the doors and stand in front of the screen and demand they turn the goddamn thing down.

"There are laws," our mother says, "you hear me," she says, "laws."

The pot bounces up and down off the floor, but no one turns the volume down.

"Maybe because the pounding of the pot plays right into a scene of the film," Louisa says. "Maybe they are showing a film about a crazy woman hammering her way with pots through walls and floors to escape."

* * *

Louisa has to play in a concert at school. When she comes back from the concert she's more beautiful than ever. Her hair is in tendrils from the hot lights and sweat and her cheeks and lips are red, her eyes darting and quick from all the excitement.

"Play for us what you played," our mother says, but Louisa groans and says, "No, I'm too tired."

Louisa goes to bed and then our mother and I and Jody are quiet, listening for music, as if Louisa had carried the whole concert home with her on her hair and her skin and her clothes and now it's playing back to us while she drifts off to sleep, filling our house with Mozart, Vivaldi, Bach.

Can you imagine the slut having to do it? Having to look through all the Smiths downtown? Her finger stopping at each one and then dialing, waiting for someone to answer, having to say, "This is your father's girlfriend, do you know where he is?"

A drink by her, a tinkling one with lots of ice, and a tinkling bracelet on her wrist, the tennis kind. Wrinkles like scythes at her temples, curving down, slicing straight for her eyes. There are black things chipped in among the blue and green, so the eye seems scattered, once exploded, colors now caught in her iris, orbiting the black hole of her pupil. Her eyes dart and search the flimsy page.

"Everyone's a goddamn Smith," she says out loud. She stands, walks around the room holding the princess phone, taking it with her to the kitchen, the window, the mantel. She waits for answers. Some Smiths answer and they sound like Garcías or Lopezes instead. The ones that sound like girls interrupted while counting ceiling tiles she asks, "Is this Cal's girl?" When she gets one, finally, she says nothing. She takes a drink of her drink, a loud one so the girl knows she's still there. The girl can hear the tinkle of her bracelet and the tinkle of her ice. The girl knows who it is.

"Is this Cal's girl?" the girl says.

"It's Cal's girlfriend," the slut says.

"Just a minute," the girl says. The girl puts the phone down on the floor. The dog comes to sniff it. The girl gets up and changes the channel on the TV. She goes around the dial more than twice, she stops it at a commercial. A swirly frosting ad for cake. The girl picks up the phone again. The frosting is chocolate spread thickly like whitecaps in a choppy sea. The girl holds the receiver to her ear and waits.

"Are you there?" the slut says.

"No, I'm here," the girl says.

"Is this Louisa?" the slut says.

"Jody," the girl says. The girl is not Jody. The girl is really Louisa.

"I've got a question, Jody," the slut says.

"Hold on," Louisa says. She hangs the phone by its cord off the arm of the chair. "Come here," she says to the dog. "Too tight?" she says, and she lifts the collar off the dog and scratches the dog's neck, the dog letting her head go limp in Louisa's lap. Louisa picks the receiver back up.

"Oh, am I interrupting something important?" the slut says and rolls her exploded eyes to her ceiling, turning a glare to the tin tiles. Louisa puts gum in her mouth and starts to chew.

"I've got a question," the slut says.

"Question away," Louisa says.

"Have you, by any chance, seen your father?" she says.

"My father," Louisa says, like the beginning of a story she is going to tell about her father. "My father was a Cretan. My mother was a spy," Louisa says.

"What's that?" the slut says.

"The beginning of something," Louisa says. The slut goes into the bathroom. She likes the sound of her shoes on that particular tile floor. She walks around in little circles and then she puts the lid down and takes a seat.

"Are you in the john?" Louisa says. Louisa knows the slut calls the bathroom the john. "Is that the john?" Louisa says.

"Never mind," the slut says. "Have you or haven't you seen your father?" she says.

"When?" Louisa says.

"I don't know when, lately," the slut says.

"Oh, lately," Louisa says.

"Well?" the slut says.

"I'm thinking who I've seen," Louisa says. "Lately," she adds. "There was Jesús, just a little while ago."

"Not all the names, please," the slut says. "This is difficult for me. You understand," she says.

"Have you looked in the kitchen?" Louisa says, "or are you still in the john?" she says.

"He's not here, anywhere, for days," the slut says. "Can't you see?"

"He's left you, then?" Louisa says.

"Is that what you think?" the slut says. "What if he's hurt? Aren't you worried? He's your father for chrissakes,

83

Jody," she says.

"Check your wallet," Louisa says.

"What?" the slut says.

"Check it," Louisa says.

The slut puts the phone down. She gets her slim crocodile wallet tanned black. After she opens it she gets back on the phone and says, "I can't believe you made me do that."

"Well," Louisa says.

"I can't tell," the slut says. "He's your father. The things you say," the slut says. "Aren't you ashamed?"

"What about the plastic?" Louisa says. "The Amex and all that. Check it too." The slut checks.

"Here, all here," she says. "Now what?" Louisa passes the phone to Jody.

"Hello?" Jody says.

"Who's this?" the slut says.

"Louisa," Jody says.

"Oh, what happened to Jody?" the slut says.

"I don't know what happened to Jody," Jody says. "I thought you were looking for our father, not Jody."

"Have you seen him?" the slut says.

"Did he really steal from you?" Jody says.

"No. I don't know. Everything seems to be here. Listen, as I told Jody already, I'm in a difficult position here."

"Are you on the john?" Jody says.

"Listen, I haven't seen your father, you hear me, your own father, for days now. No note, no telephone call, not any kind of word at all. I'm, frankly, quite worried," the slut says.

"Louisa, are you there?" she says.

"I'm here," Jody says.

"You see, really quite worried. What are we to do?" the slut says. Jody is now letting two of her mice climb up and down her arms while she talks on the phone. The receiver is held between her bent neck and shoulder. It drops to the floor when she giggles, when the mice run out to the edge of her fingertips she always giggles. Louisa picks up the phone.

"Jody here," Louisa says.

"Jody? All right. It doesn't matter who. Listen, we've got to do something, fill out some kind of report. Go to the police," the slut says. The slut is standing in the hall now. She stands and looks down the stairwell as she talks. "Because, you see, he's not coming. He's not here," the slut says. The slut holds out her hand over the empty space above the stairwell, emphasizing.

"He's not missing from here," Louisa says. "He doesn't live here."

The slut laughs and then wipes her nose with her hand. "Jody, you're a smart girl. Aren't you a smart girl? I'll answer for you, because I know. Think how it looks. I'm in the station. The girlfriend. I'm telling the fat cop behind the desk I can't find my lover, that he's been gone for days. Are you with me? And you, now you be the fat cop behind the desk, Jody, you tell me what the fat cop says to me, the girlfriend," the slut says. "'Lady, what makes you think he didn't get up and leave you?' That's it, that's what you, Jody, say, if you, Jody, are the fat cop. Forms need to be filled out, Jody. That's what I'm saying," the slut says. The slut is back in her kitchen now. She takes a dirty tall glass that holds the remnants of gin and an old lemon and she tosses the gin into the sink and then fills the glass with tap water and puts the old lemon back in the glass and then she drinks. Louisa hears her swallow.

"Lady, what makes you think he didn't get up and leave you?" Louisa says.

"That's exactly what he'd say," the slut says.

"Lady, what makes you think he didn't get up and leave you?" Louisa says again.

"You want me to answer that? Is that what you're doing?" the slut says. "I'll answer that. No, wait, why should I answer that? You're smart, you Smith girls, but you're also cruel. But never mind that now. We've got work to do. You've got to get up here. A.S.A.P. All right? Do you hear me. Hello? Hello?" Louisa goes through the channels again. A nature show shows dying elephants searching for water, their trunks looking stretched out and dragging on the ground.

"Uptown. Take the bus. Take whatever you take. The subway, it's faster," the slut says.

"I can't watch this," Jody says to Louisa. "It's not my cup of tea." She walks back to her room, her arms out in the style of zombies, her mice running on them.

"A cab, I think," Louisa says, "is what you want us to take. It's what will get us there faster. Pay for our cab, meet us at the curb with your wallet ready. And victuals," Louisa says, "buy some in advance. We like hamburgers. Two apiece."

"When are you leaving? Leave now," the slut says.

"Remember, it's your father," and then she says, "I'm hanging up now. I'll expect you no later than twenty minutes from now. That's plenty of time. Isn't that plenty of time? Jody? Twenty minutes?"

"One hour," says Louisa, "you'll need it to get the burgers." She hangs up the phone and then she says to me and Jody, "It's all right when it's bugs dying or being eaten, their hairy legs being torn off, but when it's these drooping elephants they show, I can't watch it. Who can watch this?" She turns off the television and leans back in her chair and closes her eyes.

Imagine the slut now still holding her hand on the receiver of the phone. Frozen in the act of putting it down and ready to pick it up all at once. Call the girls back. Tell them one thing more. Tell them anything to get them to really come, because she doesn't think they really will. Except, ah yes, the food. They will come. And she lets go of the phone and pulls takeout menus from the night table by the side of the bed. She jiggles the drawer, the paper menus are caught up under whatever runners or knobs there are that make a drawer slide. "Oh, damn it," she says. She yanks harder, and her tennis bracelet gets caught up on a hook and breaks, falling with a jingle.

She stands and looks out the kitchen window. There is nothing out there, no person, only trees in the dark, maybe a wind off the river.

The girls eat in the station. Blood drips on their hands. The cop is not fat, too thin maybe, his chin meant for putting up in the air, his elbows for getting by in crowds, angled for jabbing.

"Shauna," she says, and maybe he's Irish because he spells it S-E-A-N-A-H and she corrects him, taking the pen from him, warm from where he held it.

"And them," he grabs the pen back to point.

"Direct relations," she says, "his daughters. Come along, girls. Come give your names."

The cop has a few questions. He wants them to name places their father might be.

"We don't know," Louisa says. "Have you got a globe?" The cop does not. He only has maps of uptown, huge ones in plastic hanging from wooden sticks on a rack.

"So when can we expect the dogs to be unleashed?" the slut says.

"There are no dogs," he says.

"I know," she says. "When will you start the search, I mean?" The girls have gone outside. They have two jump ropes they uncoil. She gives the cop a photo. Cal at Easter, a roast duck in the foreground. Crystal and eyelet linen. They start the jump ropes circling.

"The search is going on, right now," the cop says. "For the father of those girls," he says, his chin pointing out the precinct's glass doors. The girls now double-dutching, skipping over what could be a mirror image of the nighttime sky, a sidewalk sparkling under street lamps lighting all the flecks of starry rock and sand.

John is in for his hip. That's what the other hot dog men say. One pulls out a hot dog from his bin and says, "This is how long the metal rod will be that will go in his body."

John comes back weeks later looking like a woman. Sharp bones protrude on his thin wrists. His hair is longer, gray and brushing his shoulders, blowing in breezes off the river. He's gentle with his tongs, the hot dogs gingerly laid between slit buns.

"I didn't come to visit you in your hospital," I say.

"No one did," he says. "I didn't tell them where I was. I'm wearing a goddamn dress with no back—all of me for whoever out there to see, I want visitors? No," he says. "I read books."

"What books?" I ask.

"Books I've already read, the ones I still like."

"What about TV?" I ask.

"The nurse was always in the way, her pointy hat cutting off all up to the tits of the broads," he says.

"My father's gone," I say.

"Your fucking father never leaves you," he says. "Fathers hang around your neck and bruise up your skin all your life long. You know that," he says. And then a man comes to buy a hot dog. He wants onions on his hot dog, but John hasn't got any. Not today.

"What? No fucking onions? What more fresh hell is there in store for me today?" the man says and he leaves, shaking his head and not buying a hot dog.

"There's your horsie," John says and points toward the park at my stallion who's letting his shit drop from his rear on the pavement.

"Nice, I'm glad you pointed that out," I say.

"Here, take him this," John says and he reaches in and pulls up a hot dog and I grab it and run across the street with it dripping and palm up I put the dog under the stallion's nose and he eats it and then I run, the cop yelling after to me to never ever feed a police horse and that next time he sees me he'll... "Do what?" I yell back at him over my shoulder as I'm running. "Arrest me? Arrest me?" I yell. But the cop isn't going to let this go, and he spurs the stallion and he's trotting after me and I'm running now up the avenue and I'm still yelling, "Arrest me? Arrest me?"

I get to Rena's house all out of breath and with legs that don't want to make it up the stairs but want to sit on the lower bottom step and shake while I hold them and slap them so they'll be still. I'm still slapping when the Hells Angel boyfriend comes down.

"Hey," he says and "Hey," I say back.

He's wearing leather pants and boots and a leather jacket and leather strings braceleted around his wrists and strung as loops through his nose and leather gloves with the fingers cut off and a leather belt and leather straps on his leather boots and he smells like leather and he pats me on the head as he passes me and goes out the door. His hair is long like my hair, and just washed and brushed it seems to float up as he walks out into sunlight.

Up at the house Rena's not home but Rena's mother is there and she is shooting basketballs. She's got a soft foam ball and a net above her bathroom door and she's shooting from her barstool and Muy Hombre's retrieving for her, bringing her the ball back in return for slices of orange American single-wrapped cheese. The empty plastic wraps are all over the floor by her barstool and Muy Hombre's skidding on them when he runs back to her with the foam ball in his mouth.

"I just want to lie down," I tell her and head for the couch, but she takes my hand and says it's time I had my ears pierced. She doesn't have ice so she picks at the clogged-up freezer compartment with a screwdriver and holds the white ice with ridges formed in it from the freon tubes on my lobe. The needle goes in and I faint.

I wake up with Muy Hombre standing over me, the foam ball still in his mouth, and Rena's mother's off by the sink saying, "Hold on, sweetie, you've had yourself a fall," but she's not helping to pick me up and instead she's knocking more ice from the freezer, intent on my other lobe.

"Let's do this one lying down," she says, "so we don't have you falling again."

"Big deal," my mother says when she sees my ears. "Mine were pierced when I was a baby."

The new holes in my ears throb, clog, and crust. As I sit in Wood, I can feel them leaking, the fluid running down the side of my neck. We are onto mailboxes. Mr. Lenin shows us how to burn our names into the wood with a penlike tool that plugs in the wall. But the boys have found they can burn their names in their arms with the tool and the room starts to smell like their cooking flesh.

"A mailbox, that's useful," our mother says and she hangs it on the wall by her chair and when her ashtrays are full and when her empty soda cans are full of ashes, she puts the ashes in the mailbox along with her twisted empty cigarette packs. Jesús hands us our mail anyway, so we have never used a mailbox. I tried telling this to Mr. Lenin before I started making mine, but he didn't understand.

"It's for mail, you can always use it," he said.

"Fuck, forget the mailbox," I said and I started to leave the room and right before I did I turned around and looked at him and said, "I hate wood."

There go the hot dog men, I say when I see them get ready to leave, their umbrellas tied shut with frayed rope or ripped sheet, their aprons stained and wet from a hard day of sloshing and tonging around in their greasy bins. Their socks in their sandals stained also, stray bits of sauerkraut dangling on the many-times-mended cloth at the toes, drying there, moving jerkily as the hot dog men move, getting ready to go, closing up cart. They leave like they're escaping, one by one, silent and quick, leaning over their handles, looking left and right without moving their heads. Any minute ready to crouch down behind their carts to protect themselves from a rain of shrapnel or a spray of bullets.

It is night, the middle of the night, and Jochen the German artist neighbor has hanged himself and the police are in our hallway again and the men in white coats can't fit the gurney in the elevator and they have to use our stairs and they come through our house and wheel our neighbor through.

"I've already cleared it," my mother says to the men in white coats, almost proud. She means the house, she's cleared the furniture for our brother to come through.

Jochen worked in oils that stained everything he touched. I can't see him under the sheet, but I can see his hand, the blue and black and red-stained fingertips, the half-moon nails black as night. My mother reaches out and grabs his hand. "Jochen," she says.

The men carry Jochen down the stairs, his paint-stained hand now showing from under the sheet, as if he is reaching out to the wall, still trying to paint on flat surfaces.

* * *

"I hear Jochen walking through the house at night," our mother says. "I hear his footsteps." We say we hear him too. We hear the floorboards creaking in the middle of the night. We smell the oil paint.

"He's watching over us," our mother says. Days later we find money in our hallway sealed to a filing cabinet with a glob of red paint.

"Jochen left us this," she says. I buy food for a week with the money and give the cashier at the E & B the bills with red paint still on them.

My mother thinks of things to do for him. Light church candles, name a star, send money to somewhere. She has one of his small unframed paintings he gave her years ago. She takes it to her office and hangs it in her cubicle. Coworkers tell her what they see in it, all sorts of things. Men without heads. Horses striking. Two moons. The cleaning people spray it with cleanser each night. It seems to change color and crack. My mother says she never saw anything in the painting before, but now in the cracks she sees bison.

"Surely bison," she says, "I've seen them before." We ask where and she says, "Merde, I can't remember where."

She tells us things she did not do in France. She never wore underclothes, like they do in this uptight country, she never bathed every day, she never ate cereal for breakfast. She can go on and on, there was so much not done over there, she says. She says she wishes she could turn around, turn her head back and see it all before her. The sea and the esplanade and the streets and the sardine vendors. She would breathe it in, she says, and then step into it and shut the door behind her. "Click," she says. She shuts a door we can't see, grasping a handle that is just the air in our house.

Tallulah Bankhead's lost at sea. She's wearing fine jewels. Her wet hair still holds a curling iron's wave. Our mother says, "That's me, that's how I feel," and she points to the TV, to Tallulah Bankhead who's now bending over boatside trailing her ringed fingers through misty waters of the set.

"We're supposed to want her dead," Louisa says.

"Poor Tallulah, misunderstood," our mother says.

Jody sits in the chair with her down coat still on, having come from a walk with the dog. She's been sick all spring and won't take the coat off. Its orange nylon is stained all down the front, its holes patched with peeling silver squares of duct tape. She snorts, moving mucous along her passages, all throughout the movie. We give her dirty looks and then we throw things. Every time she snorts she gets a paperback or a pillow or a cat thrown at her.

"I'm sick!" she says.

"Well, get over it," Louisa says.

She sleeps with the coat on, over her nightgown under her covers. We hear her snort and cough all night.

"She was born too young, her lungs barely formed, that's why," our mother says and then she says, "Was that Jody?" when she hears a noise.

"Yes," I say. "Go back to sleep."

"She's like Beth in *Little Women*," Louisa says from her bed. "She'll die this spring."

"Don't say that," our mother says.

"Am I Jo?" I say.

"No, you're Tiny Tim," Louisa says. My mother and Louisa laugh from their beds. I hit my mother in the back. She is smoking in bed and the cigarette falls from her fingers and onto the sheet.

"Oh, merde," she says and bangs at the mattress, putting out the burning ash.

Then my mother starts to cough her smoker's cough and Jody starts to cough her sick cough and Louisa and I join in with fake coughs.

The loft next door where Jochen lived is about to be shown. The landlord's left the door open for cleaners. On the table that is really an old door over sawhorses are paint cans and brushes and dribbled dry paint and a dropcloth and a bell and a book and a candle. The candle was melted at the bottom. It stands at a slant in a pool of its wax. The bell has paint on it, the clapper is gone. The book is the Bible, a copy in German. Some pages torn out and used to wipe paint from his brushes are crumpled in balls on the floor.

They've left the rope, but not the loop. I hold onto the cut rope, pull myself up, a one-armed chin-up. The pipe it's tied to spills dust in the air.

His paintings are all over the house. I can't see anything in them. It's hard to tell if they're finished or not. He has even painted over windows and on the stove. Like spillover from boiling pots, splashes of paint stain the oven door and hide the numbers on the range's dials.

There are pictures of his children, German children on the freezer box. Blond and blue-eyed. The photos hang by magnets. Jochen painted the frames with pictures of elephants dancing in tutus and giraffes wearing bowties.

Do the German children know their father is dead? Do the German children sit quietly in a park with pigeons by a fountain in a German town, their heads lowered, their mother telling them the transatlantic news?

I take the pictures of his children and put them in a cigar box. I take them to John. I tell John, "Here, tape them to your hot dog cart," and he does, saying there are children from where he comes from who look the same, their hair the color of the sun, their eyes blue like sky.

Before we go to school we watch our mother put her makeup on. First the powder on the face, then the eyeliner below the eye and above on the lid an exaggerated stroke like the sweeping end of a Chinese character drawn with black ink and brush. Then a layer of blue and violet and pink eyeshadow.

The eyebrows wetted with a licked finger and then darkened with pencil. The bar of blush on the cheeks and then the lining of the lips. She shakes her hand back and forth, a ritual, freeing the brush of her plastic lipliner stick. Don't we close our eyes, us girls, lean back our heads and listen to the shaking, breathe deeply, smell her L'Oréal, her Givenchy. She takes the Maybelline, licks the point and then dots her cheek with a beauty mark. She teases up her hair, then fastens it back down with bobby pins she's been holding in her teeth.

When she's finished we grab our books and stand in the hall, buzzing the elevator, waiting for Jesús to bring us down to the street. On the other side of the wall we can hear our brother snoring in his bed. He sleeps on his box spring now and when he turns we can hear the springs twang like an instrument he is just learning to play with the sharp pointed bones in his hips.

Rena goes to Puerto Rico. She writes that she has met her real father for the first time.

She sends oranges. She has a boyfriend named Ramón. He has given her bracelets of shark's teeth and a necklace to match. She saw angelfish and starfish. Ramón's got a brother, Realidad.

"That's Reality," she writes. If I came to visit her, Realidad and I could be boyfriend and girlfriend. "Will you come to visit me?" she asks. "PR is hot, baby. We sleep under nets. You will never guess how old Ramón is. Ramón is nineteen," she writes. "Realidad is not so old." Her father locks himself up and paints during the day and eats dinner with her at night. They go to bars and she dances with his friends. They are dark and have hair on their backs. She will miss the coconuts when she returns, she knows.

"Eat the oranges by slicing a hole in the top and then sucking out the juice," she writes.

I cannot go to PR.

"Here," our mother says, "take this instead," and she digs up a frilly blue negligee from a barrel where we store our clothes. I put it on over my clothes. "I wore that in the hospital with your sister," our mother says. "I craved corn flakes, not pickles," she says.

I show John the frilly negligee. I still wear it over my clothes. He asks me to twirl, and I do, holding out the filmy skirt of it while he takes pictures of me.

"Beautiful," he says. "Here," John says, and gives me quarters, "buy yourself an ice cream."

"I'll take another hot dog," I say. I stay with John until the end of the day when he folds down his umbrella and says he's going home.

My brother smokes pot like cigarettes. He rolls them and then puts them in hard packs and keeps them in the pocket of his robe. He flips the pack open when he wants one, and the way he likes them is chained, one right after the other while he watches the soap operas with me. He doesn't want histories now, he stops me when I start to explain their desperate lives. His heavy-lidded eyes almost closed throughout the show, I sometimes throw a book at him to wake him up and he laughs, not with his voice, just his chest slightly shaking up and down and a smile on his lips.

I walk to see John and all I see is his cart. I think this is it, he's gone and I'll have to trundle the fucker of a cart back downtown all by myself. I'll have to keep it in my hallway for him until the next day and then get up early, join the other hot dog men in the morning, slip into formation and then walk with them and walk their foreign walk to the park and see if John has shown up by then. But John is not gone, he is on the side of the cart, kneeling down and fixing a tire.

"That's new," I say. He's wearing a hat. The paper kind the

boys wear who serve at the fast food.

"You like?" he says.

"Sure," I say. "Where'd you get it?"

"Same place I get all of these," he says and pulls on his apron skirt.

"None of the other hot dog men are wearing them. Maybe it doesn't say Sabrett. Maybe people won't want to buy your hot dogs because they think it won't taste like the hot dogs they're used to getting," I say. John sits up.

"You think so?" he says. "What do you know what says Sabrett?"

"Fuck, I don't," I say.

"You don't know anything. You're a kid," he says.

I nod my head. I look at his bloodshot eyes and wonder if it affects what he sees, everything covered by a veil of red lace that his hands can't ever lift.

At home, I look in the refrigerator. There's nothing in it but old lettuce leaves, so old they're dried to the glass shelf and can't even be peeled off.

My mother calls from work. I can hear her typing while I talk.

"Are you typing what I'm saying?" I say.

"No, I'm working," she says.

"I bet I can make you type what I say," I say. I say, "Dear Mr. Elbow, renege, please advise, cordially, at your earliest convenience."

"Oh, merde," my mother says, "are you happy now, I made a mistake."

"Happy," I say.

"I'll be home late," she says.

I dial my father. He's been missing for weeks and I think maybe he's come back. I imagine him shopping at Balducci's, buying persimmons and shiny egg-white baked bread. But there's no answer. I slam the phone receiver down on the floor. It bounces. I do it again. There is now a nick in the floorboard. I don't put the receiver back in its cradle. I sit in the chair, my mother's chair. It gets dark, but I don't turn the light on. The recorded voice tells me to hang up the phone. Then it finally stops and the phone is now quiet. I look through the drawers in my mother's table, the one with all the burn marks on it. In the drawers are ripped photos. All the photos are of my mother with her missing arm around where my father used to be, but I can't find the halves with him in them.

I dial my mother.

"I'm at work," she says.

"I know, I called you," I say.

"I'm working," she says.

"Where's Dad?" I say. "Where's the rest of the photos you ripped in half?"

"What photos?" she says.

"The photos with your arm around him and his arm around you," I say.

"I can't talk," she says. "Goodbye." She hangs up the phone.

"Let's find the photos," I say to my sisters. We turn all the lights on in the house. We start with the barrel we use to store old clothes. In it are fishing waders whose rubber is cracked, and dull-pointed ice skates, but no photos of our father. We pull down boxes from shelves in the storage room. Empty cockroach egg sacs cascade around our heads. We shake our hair and scream, but we still look for the photos. We get our brother to help. He can reach the upper shelves. There are pictures of my father in Illinois with his pet collie. There are pictures of France, the wave curl black and the surf break white and frothy, coming up the shore.

"Look how young," we say when we see the photos. Our mother waving. Our father with a smile. My brother's silk robe gets caught in a space heater stored on a lower shelf, it rips from the hem upward, a long gash threatening the fire breathing dragon.

"Oh, fucking Christ," he says. He stops helping us. He sits down right away, with a needle and thread and starts to repair. We cannot reach to put the boxes back on the upper shelves. Our mother comes home.

"What's this?" she says, she sees the open boxes on the floor, feels the cockroach egg sacs crunching under her shoes.

"What a mess, clean it up!" she yells. She kicks at the boxes, she pulls other boxes down off the shelves. Things come tumbling out, more photos, more ripped clothes, useless lamps, their goosenecks bent over backwards, switches twisted past their limits, bulbs black and filaments broken. We smell like dust. Egg sacs and cobwebs still shift in our hair. Our mother takes a plunger, dried toilet paper still stuck to its rubber, and starts to hit at us. We run from the room, our hands above our heads to shield us from the blows.

We take showers. Later we look in on our mother. She is still wearing her clothes from work, sitting shoeless on the storage room's floor, her pocket book beside her. We bring her bread. She does not want it.

"Leave me alone," she says. We bring her a drink made with her vodka and soda. She takes it, drinks a long drink. She wipes her mouth and sets her glass on the edge of a shelf.

"What have you girls done here?" she says, and looks around the room, at all the opened boxes, their contents coming out. She picks up an old leather glove and tries to put it on but cannot wriggle into it.

"These were once mine," she says and holds it up, the shape of her young hand still visible in the leather's curled fingers.

"Help me up," she says, and we lift her by the hand and she brushes off her clothes.

"What a day at work," she says and we leave the storage room the way it is and sit with my brother. My mother takes the robe from him.

"Let me do it," she says and she undoes all his uneven stitches and starts again, her small stitches sewn from the underside almost invisible when she is done. She holds the robe up to look at her work.

"I'm incredible," she says, and she tells us to look at her work of art and we do, and we agree how marvelous, how

107

wonderful a sewing job. I get up and rub her shoulders. She screams in pain.

"Too hard," she says.

"I'm barely touching you," I say.

"I know," she says. "Just stop," she says.

We hope that he will kill himself.

"Go ahead and shoot," Louisa says to our brother over his wall, as we hear him throwing things and breaking them. He has been trying to get back together with Toffee, but she keeps saying no.

"I'll do it for you," she says through the door. "Just give me the gun." She turns to us and says she would, she would, under the chin is a good place, and she takes her fingers and sticks them up under Jody's chin and then my chin and then the dog's and says, "Right there, bang bang bang." We fall dead to the floor, all except the dog who tries to lick us back to life.

I come home from school and lock myself in the bathroom and sit on the floor and read. It is the room farthest from his room and where I cannot hear him breaking things he broke already, breaking them again. But then my mother is screaming and I come running out. My brother has smashed his fists through the glass, ruptured a vein, blood pumping through the air with the beating of his heart. My mother holds his wrist with her two hands, leading him out of his room while he cries, the snot clear and hanging long from his nose.

Fires burn in New Jersey. Our mother calls us up. "Are you all right?" she asks. We haven't been to New Jersey, no one was in New Jersey today, we tell her. "Stay inside," she says, "the smoke."

Ma Mère is sick, a blockage in her leg. She sleeps in a chair sitting up, she says there is no other way. We hear Bambi yapping in the background.

"I cannot walk my dog," she says. We bring them to the house. She stares at what's left of the burned-down trees in the empty lot below. She wears a leopard-spotted robe that she clasps with both hands at her neck.

"I'm so cold," she says, but it's hot in the house. "We are the hot little tomatoes," we tell her.

The phone rings and she says, "That's your father," every time, but it's never him. There has no been word from him at all. "When you were babies and you still cried after you were fed, he would walk you around the room for hours. He would walk you into the closet and turn the light on, he would hold up sleeves, showing you the pretty colors and the patterns of the clothes. He thought you cried because you were bored, that your brain didn't want you go back to sleep because it needed new information. Whatever he did worked. You shushed in the closet. Quiet as a mouse. He was a good father, the best," she says. Then she says she wants to go down there and points to the back lot below. There is a way through the basement, a metal-hinged thick metal door you can swing open, but it takes strength. My brother helps us, carries her down in her leopard-spotted robe while he still wears his bloodstained blue silk robe. I hold a beach chair. We get the door open partway, enough to slip ourselves through.

She sits on the beach chair. Bambi runs in the lot, gnawing on old milk cartons, barking at rats through missing bricks in the building's wall.

"This is the life," she says.

In the evenings we bring her back up. My brother holds onto one side of her and my mother holds the other side as if Ma Mère were still sitting in her chair. Ma Mère grabs my brother's hand, "Weren't you going to kill yourself?" she asks.

We used to hide the liquor, but now my mother says, "Oh, give it to her, just give it to her." And we do.

Her leg hurts her more each day. They cannot operate until she is stronger. We all wonder what that means.

"Give it time," they say. We don't know what we are giving time to. At night she moans in her chair and bangs at her leg with her fist.

"Mon livre," she sometimes says, and we know she wants *To Kill a Mockingbird* and one of us gets up to give it to her.

Some nights I think our mother is talking in her sleep, but she has just gotten up to sit by Ma Mère and speak in

French. Sometimes Ma Mère is crying, but through it all she is still hitting the blocked side of her leg. I can hear the steady thump of her fist on her thigh. Sometimes they fight, yell merdes and sacre bleus, and I wish our mother would just walk away from Ma Mère and let her die in the chair with its cushion stained by the beige Cover Girl powder that's rubbed off her cheeks as she tries to sleep leaning back, the pain making her turn her face from side to side.

Bambi runs off. He's gone and we all have to look for him. We cross through the lot with its skinny pale burnt trees and stick our heads down into the basements of the other buildings. We walk the streets in our neighborhood, calling, "Bambi, Bambi." Our mother tells us Bambi probably won't work, what will instead is Mon Cherie, so now we are all walking down the streets calling "Mon Cherie, Mon Cherie," and there is still no sign of the bulging-eyed dog.

Jody comes home mugged. She was down in our hallway and two guys came up from behind her and held a knife and then they slashed her down coat with the knife before they left her. The feathers are all over and some are stuck to the tears on her face. She's coughing so much she can't tell the story and we sit her down and more feathers fly up around her and we wave them away and kneel by her chair and ask what the hell happened.

After that we are everywhere with the dog. No one leaves the house without her and she goes on so many walks that she slinks away when one of us gets up to leave. I bring her with me to visit John, and we balance hot dogs on her nose and she goes cross-eyed and salivates and finally I give her the okay and she tosses them up in the air with the end of her nose and catches them in her mouth, swallowing them whole. Fuck, what a dog.

John wants me to sit on his lap, but the dog growls and bares her teeth when he gets near me, even after he's given her all those hot dogs.

"Don't bring her again. It's bad for business," he says. He makes to hit her with his tongs and she rears, her ferocious bark turning heads from as far away as the fountain, turning the head of the stallion, stopping him up short and pricking his ears. I see his tongue glide over the brass bit, back and forth, as if he wants to swallow it or spit it out, a tic brought on by all the pulling of reins and the jabbing of hard boot heels.

I signal the dog. Just one hand raised in the air by one of her family, and she knows to stop, to sit and obey. But I still hear a deep growl come up from inside her, like the far-off roar of the subway.

Rena's missing weeks of school. The boys all ask me when she'll be back and I tell them I don't know. Her letters are about roosters she hears in palm trees at night, their scuttling keeping her awake.

* * *

Our brother's in his room again with the gun. I climb the ladder and look down over at him. He's got the gun spread across his knees.

"That's a small gun," I say. "Isn't it?" I say. "Isn't that the one Grandpa hunted rabbits with? Maybe it's only big enough to kill a rabbit and not big enough for bigger things. Maybe it's the wrong kind of gun," I say and then I get down off the ladder and leave my brother alone.

If we leave Ma Mère alone in the house, she falls from her chair, on her way to where we don't know, still wearing her leopard-spotted robe.

Our mother straps Ma Mère to the back of her chair with brightly colored belts from all our different bathrobes. We think about strapping her head back too, because it falls so often to the side and onto her shoulder or forward when she's sleeping or drunk, but our mother thinks that would be too cruel. "We just don't want her to stand up and hurt herself while we're out during the day," she says.

When I'm alone again with Ma Mère I ask her to tell me more about my father, but she's not hearing now. Her head is leaning back over the top of her chair. Her mouth is partly open and her eyes are closed.

I find a picture of our father. One our mother didn't cut in half, probably because I'm in it. I'm maybe two years old, sitting on his lap. He's got his arms around me, his hands holding the bottoms of my bare feet. I look like any moment

I could stand up and he would help me spring into the air and I would do a perfect gainer, a graceful headlong dive.

I made a few ten-cent copies on the machine at Woolworth's, using change I found at the bottom of the fountain in the park. For a few nickels and dimes, I can always count on the fountain, where tourists think the dirty, wrapper-filled water can make a wish come true.

With scissors I cut out the part of the copies that have the image of myself and then I write "missing" on the bottom of the pages. I leave our phone number to call and I also write "reward," thinking no one would bother to call if I didn't offer one. I think about giving away the TV as a reward, or maybe even two or three of Jody's mice.

I don't have scotch tape, just band-aids. I use those to hang the signs to lampposts. After I hang up the signs, I go home and sit by the phone. It doesn't ring. I go out and check the signs. Maybe someone had seen him but didn't have a pen to write down the phone number so they tore down the sign. If that happened then I'd know I was closer to finding him. The signs are still up though, the band-aids doing a stellar job.

The doctors say not yet when they see Ma Mère. They take her blood pressure, roll up the faded sleeve of her leopard-spotted robe. They ask our mother what Ma Mère is talking about because she speaks in French.

"She's telling you her dreams," our mother answers.

"Ask her if this hurts," they say, pressing on her leg.

"She says there are things that hurt worse but she has never felt them," our mother translates.

When she's sleeping and I come home from school and no one else is there, I tell her about John the hot dog man. How he lost a tooth and it fell into one of the bins. He rolled up his nubby sweater's sleeve and plunged his hand in after it, then he said the water's burning hot, that he now knows how the poor hot dogs feel being boiled to death. She doesn't wake up and it's not until our mother comes home that she wakes up and asks in French for more wine or more gin.

My brother is watching a soap opera and separating pot leaves from seeds with a playing card, getting ready to roll himself a joint in the cardboard lid of our Monopoly game.

"Fuck," I say. I turn the TV off.

"Leave it on," he says. "Or I'll beat the crap out of you."

I laugh. "Go on," I say. I stand facing him with my arms crossed, blocking his view of the television.

"I'm serious," he says, but he keeps doing what he's doing, then tilts the Monopoly cover and I can hear all the little tiny pot seeds rolling along the cardboard.

"Why don't you get off your ass and go find him?" I say.

"Find who?" he says.

"Dad," I say.

Now it is he who laughs. His eyes become slits again, his chest shakes. The blue silk dragon bathrobe slides farther apart on his chest, revealing his smooth skin. He only stops laughing long enough to lick the rolling paper on the joint and seal the pot leaves in.

Then he says, "You're better than TV, you're a helluva

lot funnier."

"Let me have some," I say. I've never smoked pot before.

"Like hell," he says.

"I wonder where he is," I say. "Do you remember him ever saying there was some place he'd really like to go?"

"Turn the TV back on," he says.

I just sit in my chair.

He smokes his joint. The space between him and me becomes filled with a cloud of his exhaled smoke, but still I see him nod his head and then he says, "Only thing I ever heard him say was how he'd really like to get the hell out of this place."

"That's a start, isn't it? Not to look here first? Just anywhere but here," I say.

He laughs again. I can see him laughing easily this time. The cloud from his pot has cleared. "Yes," he says. "I'll start looking anywhere but here." And then he says, "You don't need pot. Your head's already fucked up. Turn the TV back on, would you for chrissakes?"

I do. I'm happy to turn it on. I'm happy to see a scene where a man for endless episodes has been out on a window ledge threatening to jump, and a woman inside cries.

In the morning our brother gets up early with us. He stands beside us while we brush our teeth and brushes his teeth too, his silky dragon robe sleeves touching our heads as we bend down to spit and rinse. He is going to look for our father.

"First the racetrack," he says and he comes home later that day saying he saw parts of our father. Another man with the same bald head. Another man with the same hunched back. A woman with his eyes. A lot of people with his shoes. Some with his smell, or it was just the popcorn machines. Some with his thumb, curled around programs, wide enough to cover strings of printed words and complicated racing terms. Some who he will someday be, trundling their IVs alongside them, heading for a cheap seat, stopping along the way, turning thrown tickets with their toes on the ground, hoping to find winners another man missed.

He goes back the next day, thinking he will now find the whole of our father. The sounds of the calls of the races like blood in his ears. He admires the board, its fast blinking lights and ever-changing odds. He finds himself cheering. A horse, who would have thought, leading by lengths, bringing it on home. He favors underdogs every time.

He uses the men's room. In the mirror, at the rows of yellow-stained enamel sink bowls, he sees another man alongside him, his hands already lathered in liquid soap, trying to turn the sink handle that won't budge, going from one sink to the next that way, finding out none of them work and saying, "Shit like this always happens to me. Every time I get to a traffic light it turns red." He thinks, this man is like our father, and he goes into a stall and pulls out the roll of paper and unwinds some for the man and offers it to him, to wipe the soap off his hands. The man grabs the paper without saying a word and wipes his hands and when he's finished he throws the mass of paper on the floor, steps over it and walks out the door.

He tries the backside, sneaking past guards to shed rows in the morning when hotwalked horses are hosed down. He pulls aside blankets on beams hanging from barns, spooking horses that hit their chests against their chain webbings. A horse with one eye is the closest he has come to finding his father. The hollow socket somehow familiar, perhaps like his father's throat, the skin thin there at the base, where the pulse beats between bone.

A Puerto Rican girl at school gets pregnant. She comes to school in her father's button-down shirts and undoes a few buttons and shows us her navel which she says has popped out as far as the bulging eyes of one of those little mop dogs. I know the kind she means, the kind like Ma Mère's. A little Bambi dog eye, just one, the Cyclops of her belly.

"Comes everything with seed," Mr. Lenin says. We are building wooden birdhouses.

"Rats come," says the pregnant Puerto Rican girl. She has seen them shimmy up the brick of buildings, so many you'd think it was ivy, but it's just what the realtors call Lower East Side charm, crawling rats instead of climbing ivy. She is afraid for her not-yet-born child's cheeks. The rats might think they're chunks of cheese and bite them.

"I'd like to build a wooden trap instead, if it's all right with you," she says to Mr. Lenin. Others of us do too, with guillotine doors that slide down when the rats step on a dowel to get to the seeds. When she is nearly due the class gives her a shower and she receives our wooden rat-traps in the shapes of birdhouses tied with yellow and pink ribbons. We all sign a card. "May your baby's cheeks never be chewed." She cries and hugs us and lets us feel her kicking baby. "If everything comes for seed," she says to me, "then maybe a little seed could bring your father home." I shake my head. "A trap then?" she says. She turns to Mr. Lenin. "What would it take to build one big enough for a man?"

"More wood," Mr. Lenin says, while he stands at the mirror hung in the closet of the classroom cutting his long black nose hairs with a tiny saw blade.

The next day Mr. Lenin opens the door to the supply room.

He points at me. "Come, I show you," he says. I point at myself. "Me?" I say.

"Yes, come," he says.

I walk into the supply room. There's metal shelves stacked with different lengths of wood. A lot of wood.

"When you are ready. I help you build trap. The one for a man," he says. "I know how to do it. But don't tell principal." He takes down a huge piece of wood from a top shelf. "We start with this," he says. He takes my hand and places it over the wood. I glide it back and forth, feeling sawdust, the powder of the wood.

"I once wanted to build same trap when I was your age," he says.

Finally, I get a phone call. Someone saw my sign.

"I found your dog," a man says:

"My sign is for a man. My dog's right here," I say. It's true, our dog is sleeping in the corner with one of the cats sleeping curled up between her legs.

"What's my reward?" the man says.

"The reward is you get to keep the dog," I say.

"That's fucked up," the man says. "I should report you to the humane society."

One night we all wake up because Ma Mère's standing at the window, pointing at a bum wandering on the street. She is calling for our mother, asking out loud in French if she remembers her father and our mother answers of course she remembers her father, and Ma Mère draws our mother near and puts a hand on our mother's shoulder and says in French, "Vois tu? There he is, wave to him," she says. Our mother waves to him and puts her arm around Ma Mère's waist and the two of them watch the bum, reeling, drunk, trying to make his way up the street.

In the morning the bum is at our breakfast table.

His name is Manolo and he is not our mother's father.

"But he is hungry and we should help him," our mother says and Ma Mère, from her chair in the living room, says, "Oui, he is hungry," so we have to let him stay and our mother finds some of my brother's shorts that he never wears and she gives them to Manolo.

"Call him Uncle," our mother says a few days later.

"Uncle?" we all cry out.

"He could be yours, he looks so much like my father," she says and she makes him special meals cooked with saffron that stains our wooden spoons yellow.

"That's what it does to your insides too," Louisa says, holding up the yellowed spoons, showing us how we are yellow-bellied.

Manolo sleeps in an old car parked on the street, saying he doesn't mind it there, especially since the weather's warming up. The car doesn't run and every other day Manolo puts it in neutral and we help push it to the other side of the street so it won't be towed.

After a while, we do call him Uncle. He likes to tell us stories about Chile. Long, long stories that are mostly about women he loved and women he wished loved him back. Their eyes are all black as night and their hair soft as breezes. When he tells us the stories he outlines their figures in the air for us, dozens of big breasts and narrow waists and curved hips shaped by his hands and left standing invisible and silent all over our house.

I go to see John and he gives me a broken hot dog to eat and then he tells me to be careful, that Uncle Manolo may be a creep.

"How disgusting," I say and John nods his head but I'm talking about the hot dog he just gave me.

"Fuck, is this some kind of tail?" I ask him and I show him where I bit into the hot dog, how a string or a tail of some sort is processed into the thing. "Rat tail, must be, or big mouse," I say.

"It's just what happens sometimes to hot dogs when they're made," John says. "Eat and keep quiet. You want someone to hear you?"

John takes off his fast food hat and throws it in the garbage.

"It's falling apart," he says. He wipes his hand through his hair which shows his balding head beneath it. Sweat glistens on the rolled wrinkled skin by his neck. I've never seen him looking so hairless.

"Creeps like your new uncle make me want to go back to my country and be with my wife and kids," John says.

John says come here and he sits down and I sit on his lap and he slides his fingers up to my tits and after a minute I stand up. I think a minute's long enough for a hot dog, especially a broken one and all with a rodent tail inside.

"Go home. I'm busy," he says. But there are no customers and he's not busy, he just looks down, putting his hands around the handles on his hot dog cart, as if he's mustering energy, as if any moment he's going to run breakneck with the cart in front of him through the street, ready to crash into some bus or truck and do himself in. I don't want to leave him this way, so I tell him what my brother said, that if you're going to kill yourself you better be careful you do it the entire way, and not just half-assed so that you're stuck in a wheelchair your whole life collecting your shit in some plastic baggie. And then I go home.

"The heat has come for us," our mother says. She wears wet turban towels on her head, she once heard some swami swear that it cools the body down.

"Don't talk," she says, "there's no need for it."

Powdered, we stand akimbo, holding ourselves out from ourselves in front of dusty-bladed metal fans, the powder blowing back behind us, whitening the dog, the cats, and Ma Mère.

There's a run for ice. Louisa and I stay close to buildings, protected by their ledges, providing shade in narrow inches to the deli. The ice is all out. What remains at the bottom of the deli's glass case is just a few chips we pick up and slide down the fronts of our shirts. We search for the deli's air-conditioning vent, stand directly under it and hold our hair up from our necks, patting and waving away at our sweat.

"Can I help you ladies?" the deli man wants to know.

"We're just looking," Louisa says.

"Leave some cool air for us," he says and he shows us the door.

* * *

The bang and brattle we hear is Manolo dragging an air conditioner through the house. Where he got it, our mother doesn't want to know. They lift it to the window and turn it on and it shakes and thrums and loosens paint chips on the ledge. The dog barks and the cats arch their backs and hiss. Our mother bends down on her knees and prays, but still the cool air doesn't come. Instead there is smoke and sparks we can see through the slitted vents.

"Merde," our mother says, and she pulls the plug and opens the window and tips the air conditioner over so that it falls out the window, hitting the ground in the shrubby skinny treed lot with a loud smash.

Manolo swims in the dirty river, jumping off pylons in front of whores who are calling out Olympic scores for his leaps and dives and pointing out hazardous floating debris like a cooler and a two-by-four.

Our mother joins the whores.

"Nine-Six. Watch out for the floating can," she yells.

Later the whores get up and head back to their places on the avenue, remembering as they go to hike up their skirts, peel back their necklines, let their breasts rise to the surface.

"There were men," our mother says, "who wanted anything I left behind. One even collected my nail trimmings."

"That's too strange," Louisa says. "Did you call the cops?"

Our mother laughs, "The cops? Yes, and a cop too. I dated one. He kept a photo of me up under his hat."

"So it was everyone then? They all wanted you," Louisa says. "The butcher, the baker, the candlestick maker. You must have been lonely, you must have had no other girl-friends, just these men following you everywhere you went."

Jody and Louise and I decide to ask the Ouija game where our father is. We ask if it our father's in the country, and the Ouija spells out "r-a-i-n." We ask it if we'll see him again and it spells out "f-e-r-r-r-r-r-r-t."

"Whatever happened to 'yes' or 'no'?" Louisa says and while our fingertips are still resting on the pointer, it moves, landing on the word "goodbye."

At the E & B, I take a package of hamburger meat for our dinner and slide it into my coat. It feels cold on my chest and I think maybe it's a good thing to have it there, what if I walk outside and there's a shoot-out on the street and I accidentally get shot, then the hamburger meat may stop the bullet or slow it down and I'll live and the E & B won't press charges for my thievery because they'll be honored to say it was their pack of hamburger meat that saved the girl's life. When I get home I see the blood from the package has leaked and stained my shirt red. Our mother runs to me, looking to see where I'm cut.

"It's cow blood, fuck, leave me alone," I say and push her away and run to the shower but I've got to wait because Uncle

Manolo's already in there, singing a Chilean love song and using up all the hot water.

She married our father in a restaurant, not even a church. She wore a silver skirt and jacket and pillbox hat to match. After the ceremony, she was called to the phone, an old boyfriend wanting to know if it was too late. It was. My father took a picture of her on the phone, the wedding ring shining on her finger. She remembers being in love, but only how it made her feel and not what she felt for him. She has stored the ring in a crack in the wood in the wall, so she can pull it out with something thin and sharp if she wants to, a knife blade perhaps. He photographed just her legs, upright against the bathroom's tiled wall while she lay in the tub. Her legs slick with soapy water grew cold from posing so long. Her back began to ache. She never asked him to hurry, but just closed her eyes in the tub and imagined her legs were not really hers, and tried to stay still for him. She says she tried to stay still for too many years, that's how she always felt, as if he were making her hold a pose and it ached. She slapped herself in the face with both hands for being so stupid, the slaps leaving red welts from her wedding ring.

That's when she took it off and put it into the crack in the wood in the wall.

I'm alone with Ma Mère and I ask her what my father was like when I was small. Was he bald then too? I can't imagine him with hair. But she doesn't answer my question, instead she says, "When you were a baby, we went to the beach. He held you high above the waves because you were scared of them. The ocean was rough. I thought the both of you would be knocked down. But when he brought you back to shore there wasn't a drop of water on you."

John doesn't look like he's trying to muster up energy anymore. He's sitting on the curb, wiping his forehead with his apron. When he sees me he invites me to sit on his lap, but I shake my head. I'm hungry. I've come for some Hershey and ask for it.

"I'm all out, kid," he says.

Manolo won't get out of his car. He is drunk and unable to move. There are green and amber liquor bottles all over the floor, wedged under the gas and brake pedals, crammed into the glove box that now can't be closed. Tickets pile up under the car's wipers.

"We've got to move him," our mother says and we try, we put it in neutral and push, our mother steers, but by the time we get to the other side of the street where the parking is legal, the spaces are already taken. We keep pushing him down the avenue. The dog jumps on the hood, splaying her paws, trying to dig in with her toenails. We go crosstown.

"Let's keep going," our mother says, thinking it best to park the car right in front of the river where there are no signs restricting the parking.

"Wake up, we've given you a view of the river," our mother says through the window to Manolo. Manolo sits up, runs his hand through his hair and then looks at himself in the rearview mirror, smiling. He gets out of the car and admires his view, saying he doesn't know why he didn't think of parking here himself. He takes our mother and dances with her and the skirt of her dress flies up when he spins her on the rotting wooden pier. The heel of her shoe gets caught and she falls and she laughs and the sun is setting now and she points to it and shakes her head and looks over at us standing on the street. While she still sits where she fell, she waves and points again to the sunset, wanting us to see what she sees.

On our walk back home I count the hot dog men. There are more out there than you think. Somehow they are strategically placed on every third street corner like pieces of a chess game.

"I'm tired, let's take the bus," our mother says. But we don't have enough money for everyone to take the bus so our mother takes it alone. We jump alongside when we can, holding on the windows with our fingertips, looking in at her, smiling while she covers her mouth and tries not to laugh, and waves us back down to the ground, afraid one of us will get caught up under the wheels and be dragged crosstown.

At home we are swearing that even the poreless parts of us are sweating—eyeballs and nails and navels and tongues. We're afraid for Ma Mère, who isn't hearing, who won't answer our questions, but simply sleeps all day. At night, though, she says she doesn't sleep, saying she's too hot. When we walk by her on our way to the bathroom she says "hello" to us and sometimes lifts her fingertips in a wave. One night I stop and I sit on the floor by her chair. I don't say anything. She just starts to talk.

"That day we went to the beach, he fell asleep with you under the crook of his arm on the towel. The plan was to head back home before dinner. But we stayed. We couldn't bring ourselves to wake you. He slept with a smile on his face the whole time."

"How can you remember all of this and I don't remember any of it?" I say.

"It's not so much to remember," she says.

Our father's slut sits in the window seat at her dead parents' house, watching her brothers out back, raking leaves, throwing a ball for a dog who won't bring it back.

She sleeps in her parents' room, puts on her father's silk pajamas stored in plastic. A pattern of rulers' heads on coins. She touches a bedspread she cannot remember ever having seen before, and the curtains, she can't remember having ever seen those either. Patterns are small buds when she always thought they were full blooms. She lies on the bed. Her hands behind her head, she marvels, this is not the same ceiling. She wakes her brothers knocking on their doors, "Come look," she says, "The ceiling, who replaced it? Who painted it and changed the tiles?"

"Go back to sleep, we haven't touched the house, the house is all the same," they say.

The phone is by her bed. She picks it up and listens to its tone and then hangs it back up. She falls asleep and wakes in the middle of the night and picks up the phone again, dialing Cal's girls.

"Hello," our mother says, answering the phone quickly because she is awake and has not been able to sleep.

"Hello," the slut says. The slut pauses.

"Yes? How can I help you?" our mother says.

"I'm looking for the girls," the slut says.

"They're asleep. Are you in another country?" our mother asks.

"Another country? I don't know," the slut says.

"Because it's 2 a.m. here in the States," our mother says.

"Is it really? I'm sorry," the slut says.

"What time is it where you are?" our mother says.

"There's no clock where I am," the slut says.

Our mother lights a cigarette.

"Why is it you want the girls? Can I help you? Who's calling?" our mother says.

"I'm sorry to bother you, it being so late in the States, but I had turkey for dinner. I should say I had an awful lot of turkey. Perhaps I ate a bone. It's a filling bird. Now I'm wide awake, in pain," the slut says.

"Have you had some water then?" our mother says.

"Water? No, I hadn't thought of water," the slut says.

"Maybe you'd better ring room service, have them bring you up something, some soda maybe, to quiet your juices. Are there sodas there where you are?" our mother says. "You're not in France, by chance, are you?"

"Oh, France, oh, no, I'd like to be in France. I'd rather be in France," the slut says.

"Oh, so you've been to France? Have you been to Biarritz?"

"Biarritz is lovely, the water, the streets, the boats, I love Biarritz," the slut says.

"That's where I'm from, Biarritz," our mother says.

"How lucky, you can always go back," the slut says.

"I could go back, but the money, you know, and who is there now? My mother here and my father dead. My aunts and uncles too old to know who I am," our mother says. "I would like to take the kids to see it someday, but really, it's the money we don't have. You see, their father's left them, it's terrible, even when he was here he was not with them, he never gave them money to speak of, but now he's really left them, left no trace at all. The FBI, can you believe it, even, the FBI is involved," our mother says.

"How could he just up and leave them, without a word?" the slut says.

"If you had asked me what kind of man I had married when I married him I would never have said this kind of man," our mother says.

"You never know, do you?" the slut says.

"Yes, you're right, absolutely right," our mother says.

"He's a lout and a cad," the slut says.

"Oh, that's the truth. It is," our mother says. "People ask me if I'm lonely. Hah, lonely, I say, I'd rather be alone than with him. I've never been happier than without him. Oh, it's sad for the children, it's not fair to them, but for me, maybe it's more a godsend."

"Other women could learn from you, they should learn from you. What strength you've got, I admire that," the slut says.

"Oh, not strength. I wouldn't go overboard. I just learned a little something the big hard way," our mother says, "Are you feeling better? How are your juices? Still acting up?" our mother says.

"I think I'm better now. A lot better. After all, it was just turkey. Thank you for your time," the slut says.

"It's nothing. I'm sorry the girls are asleep, but it's late here in the States. Oh, I don't even know who's calling, who shall I tell them called? Leave your number. Or, please, call again," our mother says.

"I'll do that, I'll call again. Thank you," the slut says.

"Don't forget to call room service. Call for a soda, if they have them where you are. A ginger ale always calmed me down," our mother says, "or ask about the equivalent, there's always something like it, just with a different label or a different name."

"I'll do that, an equivalent," the slut says.

"Take care," our mother says.

"You too, goodnight," the slut says and she hangs up the phone.

Our mother sits smoking in the dark. She reaches out to pet the dog who is sitting by her chair.

"Oh, you're a good dog, aren't you. The very best," our mother says, bending down in the dark, kissing the dog's head, holding her cigarette away to the side so she doesn't burn her fur. Our mother starts to sing. "Ditez-moi pourquoi la vie est belle," she sings while she picks up her pack of cigarettes and her lighter and her drink and brings

138

them to her bedside, getting ready for bed, wiping the bottoms of her bare feet before she lies on the sheet and falls soundly asleep.

The hot dog men are stuck in the year's first snow, their tires struggling up over dirty plowed dog-pissed piles they melt with water from their bins and stomp on with the sandals they wear with socks. They knot their heads in scarves like women, the fringed ends flapping like wattles by their chins as they push and push their way up the avenue. A strong wind comes and they shield their eyes from the blowing snow with half-gloves and uncovered fingertips. I'd look for John but he is any of these men in a woolen shapeless dark coat and the scarf on the head and a hot dog cart whose steam rises upward from its bins, quickly mixing with the falling snow.

"You can forget him," our mother says, meaning our father. She is knuckling a rhythm with her hand turned over on the table and rapping one knuckle after the other. The hand twists and curls from side to side and the rhythm is flamenco. We would like to forget him, wouldn't we? A lap never sat on. His shirt buttons never played with, never pushed to make him a tiger, a bear, a monkey, a cow. Mickey Mouse never drawn. Shoulders never ridden, a neck never squeezed tight between playground-dirty, smeary sticky stick-thin little daughters' legs. A hand never held through a strawberry patch, red never creeping up the sneaker's sides, the seeds collecting in canvas tongues, leaves clogging eyelets, weaving under lace's weave, never, not ever, our father was it, just a tall man whose hand we held, the hand the right height for holding the wrong tall man's hand.

We are called about Spain.

"Malaga maybe," the cop says over the phone. "We've got a restaurant credit card receipt with what looks like his John Hancock." Are we familiar with parts of southern Spain? he asks. Not us, but our mother is. "Tell him once as a girl, but what's it to anybody now?" she says. "Their father's not at the beach, his bald head blisters in the sun. He even burns through window glass," our mother tells the cop.

"This includes another region now," the cop says. "You may also get calls from federals hereon."

School is steamy. The building warming the wool of our soggy mittens and hats and coats, wet from snowball making and snowball fights. We can hear the snow melting, dripping on closet floors, puddling out from the doors. Everything seems to be seeping out. Lunch can be smelled from first floor up to fourth. The odor of fish cakes, spawning its way up the up and down stairs to our rooms. The perfumes of teachers reaching seated pupils, spreading through the air from their slight exertions, the use of pointers, page turning and the rolling down of foreign countries' maps. Something crackly from the loudspeakers. Holiday music played so low between first bell and late bell it could be mistaken for the constant hum of private thoughts. I wait to be called. I think it will happen someday, some monitor with a piece of paper in hand for one of my teachers will have my name on it. I'll be sent down to the offices, handed the phone, my father will talk and I'll listen, static carried over the overseas lines and a slight delay clues to his distance. He'll say I'm to go to the airport, catch a plane to the south of Spain. We'll drink wine poured down our mouths in bars and bed ourselves in small boats on rocky moonlit beaches. We'll tell each other stories before sleep from our hard wood boat bottoms, then dream, safely down, the curving boatsides' briny ribcages shelters from North African winds.

Rena comes home rattling after Christmas break. Small shell bracelets reach up past elbows on each arm and earrings of small clustered periwinkles hang from her ears and coral necklaces with red branches jab at her neck. She looks like what fishermen don't want after hours spent cutting debris out of their nets. Rena weaves the shells through her long hair.

"You've been home already long enough, put your shells in boxes. Your tan is fading," Bonnie tells her and she arranges Rena's hair so that it covers her ears instead of being held behind.

Rena makes bracelets for the boys who love her. She strings a small clam shell on a strip of leather cord. The boys knot them at their wrists, wear them in their baths and the cords loosen and darken.

"Baby," she tells me, "I'm going back to live there."

"When?" I ask.

"Soon. My father wants me there. He says he'll send for me. He's sent me letters," she says. She shows me the letters. There are a lot of them, all in a stack.

"Aren't the stamps beautiful?" Rena says, but what I think is beautiful is how her father starts the letters. They all begin with "Cariña" or "Mi Amor." Sometimes he draws pictures in the margins of his pages. They are drawings of sunsets and beaches and palm trees and he has even drawn Rena and himself standing on a beach, and in the drawing he is holding her hand.

Our brother says he has seen her, the slut. Stopped at a window in midtown, looking at herself or at shoes, he couldn't tell. She looked like a bum wanting in, looking through glass at a Christmas meal, but it was only shoes in there, he says. He says he even looked himself to see if there was something else, perhaps someone motioning to her behind the pane, waving her in. But there wasn't, he says.

"She was ancient," he says, her eyes so wrinkled she must have been squinting continuously, even in her sleep, ever since they last saw her. He can't imagine any other way.

"You don't understand the ravages of time," our mother says. "Look at this," she says, and shows us her hands, holds down the veins and lets them pop back up again. "Ravaged," she says.

Our brother said hello to the slut, put his hand on her shoulder and she jumped and held her hand to her mouth and then looked at herself in the window and brought her hand down. He was amazed by her thin wrists. Had their father held them, held both of them at the same time between one hand's circled fingers? Our brother says, "She wasn't any bigger than a bird."

There's been no word of your father, she told our brother. She had written to consulates and dignitaries. She was almost learning Spanish from all the overseas communication she had received, flowered with Señoras and permisos and disculpes and finally firmados.

"Signed," she said, "it means signed."

And our brother said she reached up and gestured as if in her hand she held a pen and was signing her name to the air. Next, she was planning to go to Spain. She said she would like to go and then give up there, too. Search all she could and then stop, live in some house on the beach, cut ties to home and sit on a balcony watching fishermen string nets. She grabbed my brother's arm, he says. "Do you know what I mean?" she asked.

He wanted to take her in, anywhere. He tried the shoe store, but she held fast to the street, inviting him for coffee at the corner. She told him there were other men besides his father. "But men who were too big, or too small," she continued. "Men who coughed through the night into handkerchiefs or men who could not pick up their feet and scuffed their slippers when walking across the floor. Men who lifted their feet too high, as if always walking through deep snow. Men who woke me because their breaths through stuffed nostrils sounded like crying children or cats. Another one," she said to the waitress, before the waitress even set the first one down. Our brother tried to leave, pointed to his watch, tried to put on his coat. She grabbed his silk robe's collar, saying, "That's not what you want to hear, I know."

He was afraid for her eyes, thought they were somehow wired and lit up from the back and smoke would start to pour forth soon. He wanted to tell her to rest them awhile. He almost reached across the table and shut them himself, in the way someone would shut a dead man's eyes. She said she wouldn't try to hide it, said she couldn't, it was wearing her down. All she heard in her ears was the constant screech of trains braking, that's what it's like, she told him.

"That's what it does," she said, and she held out her hands, the fingers shaking, "an expensive manicure ruined," and showed him where the Asian girl had gone outside the boundary of cuticle, painted polish on surrounding skin instead.

It began to rain and he thought how it would stain his silk robe and so he stayed. She ordered more and more. He wanted to hold her arm down, she had coffees so many ways, au lait and American, cappuccino and decaf and also cinnamon buns and apple tarts and iced confections and soon there was no room left on the table, they used another table beside them just to hold all the plates. Finally, he did hold her arm down, no more, he said, enough, and so she stopped and began to eat. Glazed flakes of pastry hung on her lipsticked lips. She said if only his father had left some word she would not be this way, and she took her hair and held it up scrunched in her fists and she pulled on the ends to show him the way it was that she was. A letter, a note, a fingered sentence on a misted window, anything at all, and she would not be the way she was, she says.

"Let up, rain," our brother says was all he thought. She did not take her hands down from her hair until he held her by the wrists and brought them down. He thought they shook too, not just her hands, it was all of her, he could not tell from where the shaking started. She was crying now and still eating, still chewing and swallowing and then she spoke with her mouth full, saying this is how it was with most of her meals, they tasted of salt from her tears. "Come with me to Spain," she said to him. "Help me find your father," she said. He says he looked out the window when she said it. He says he pretended he did not hear her. Then she asked about his mother.

"My mother?" he said.

"I'm sorry, I'm not supposed to ask that, am I?" she said. "Shame, shame," she said, she slapped one of her hands with her other hand. And it did let up, in fact the sun shone, our brother says. Weakly through clouds that looked like more rain. He stood up and left money and she stood up too, said they could walk together and she hooked her arm through his. They passed the shoe store again and she stopped and looked in. He kept trying to walk down the street, but she held onto him, still looking in. She said she swore the shoes were already worn, showing him scuffed toes and heels already lower on one side from a wearer with a weight problem.

"Should I go in and say something?" she said laughing. "The manager should be told he's selling used shoes. Look at the stilettos, tell me they haven't been on some Latin dance floor before, or the riding boots, haven't they gouged a little horseflesh lately?" she says.

Then came the rain again, our brother said, and it came down so hard they could not see in the windows. They could barely see each other when they said goodbye, when he helped her up the steps and held her rain-soaked arm as she climbed into the bus.

The slut calls our house. "This is Louisa," I tell her, when she asks who she's speaking with.

"Is your brother there?" she asks.

"No," I say. My brother is in his room.

"Tell me," she says, "Has he said anything about coming with me to Spain?"

"Spain?" I say. He has not told me about going with her to Spain.

"We have to find your father," she says.

"Yes," I say. "He said he would go with you, but it's the money," I say. "He hasn't got enough."

"Yes, I thought that was the problem. I forgot to tell him. Tell him for me, would you, not to worry about the money. I'll take care of everything," she says.

"Sure," I say. "You'll take care of it all."

I go into my brother's room with a cup of coffee I poured into a bowl because there were no clean mugs. He's sleeping in his robe, the embroidered dragon on his back facing upward, looking like it's just touched down and is about to take my brother up in its talons and out the window and carry him to a lair somewhere beyond the roofs and tall spires of the city. I put the bowl of coffee by my brother's nose to see if the smell of it will wake him. My brother just snores into the bowl, though, rippling the brown liquid. I put the bowl of coffee down and whistle for the dog. She comes right away. I point to the bed and she jumps up on it and stands over my brother, looking at me, waiting for my next command. "Wake him up," I tell her.

What a dog. She takes her paw and puts it on his head. He mumbles in his sleep. "Again," I tell her. Now she is really pawing at his head, her nails scraping against the inside of his ear.

"Get the hell off me!" he yells with his eyes still closed, and he tries to shove her off, but she holds her ground. Then he opens his eyes and he sees me standing there.

"What do you want?" he says.

"I want you to go with the slut to Spain," I say.

"Spain, fuck," he says. "Get the dog off me," he says. I call the dog down. She stands next to me and I pet her head, then I give my brother the bowl of coffee. "A bowl?" he says and I don't say anything and he drinks it.

"I got you a free trip," I say. "And the girls," I say. "I've heard a lot about them. Not like here. They're mysterious, they're beautiful. You've never seen such darkness," I say.

"He might not even be in Spain. The feds could be wrong. I could go to Spain for nothing," he says. "He's probably right here in town. He's probably throwing back some beers across the street in the Charlie Bar," my brother says.

"The girls," I say, "can do things with their hands no other girls can."

"You're crazy," my brother says and finishes his coffee in one gulp and then puts it down on the table next to his bed. I pick up the gun that's leaning against the wall in his room and I turn the gun and point it at my brother.

"What things with their hands?" my brother says and he stands up while tying his robe tighter around his waist. He goes to his window and stands looking out at the Charlie Bar across the way. I stand next to him. I point the gun at the windows of the Charlie Bar. There's no one I can see through the windows. The Charlie Bar is closed.

My brother turns and looks at me. "That's not how to do it," he says. He raises the gun up so it fits in my shoulder. He straightens out my arm and with his foot he kicks at my foot so I spread my legs a little and stand the way a shooter is supposed to stand. When I talk, it's into the wood of the gun, into the swirls of cherry grain.

"Please go," I say.

My brother shakes his head and says, "Only thing in that Charlie Bar is a bad smell from the night before. I know," he adds, "because I was sitting there last night so loaded I was barfing into a basket of peanuts on the bar." Then he says, "I'll go. All right, I'll go."

Manolo is teaching our brother to say things.

"Dónde están los lavabos?" Manolo says.

"They all piss on the street there, teach him something useful instead," our mother says.

"Dos cervezas, por favor," Manolo says

"No," our brother tells Manolo. "Teach me right. Teach me how to say 'consulate,' how to say 'missing person,' how to say 'I'd like to file a report.'"

Manolo tells him and our brother writes the phrases down on bits of paper he safety-pins inside the lapel of his robe. Sometimes he reads them, flapping back his robe's lapel like some watch-seller on the street corner flashing us his goods.

When he's just about to leave for the plane, he picks up his bag and he can't figure out why it's so heavy until he unzips it and sees the gleam of the gun. Louisa put it in. "You never know when you might want to do yourself off," she says.

"It's do yourself in," he says and he takes out the gun and chest-passes it to her and she catches it with both hands and he says, "Is there anything else in this bag I should know about?" He leaves and Louisa aims the gun at him in our hallway and then he goes down in the elevator and from the street he waves goodbye to us at our window, Louisa still aiming the gun, telling us she has a good shot, a really good shot.

"Maybe you should have taught him how to say 'You fucking son of a bitch,' maybe you should have taught him that," our mother says to Manolo, "because that's all I'd want to learn to say if I were going over there to find him and I found him."

"'Let's dance,' 'Let's drink,' that's what you'd want to learn," Manolo says. "That's what you should learn. You hardly know it in English. Do you know it in English?" he asks our mother.

"Let's dance, let's drink," our mother says.

"No, that's not it, that's not right. Say it like you mean it," Manolo says.

"Merde," our mother says, "and now you will teach me English?"

"It could be too late. Languages are best learned young, when there's the chance you'll mean what you say later in life," he says.

Our mother is jiggling. Her leg sending the hanging light fixtures shaking. Her drink slightly sloshing, playing up the glass's lip. We are adjusting our eyes. The evening through our skylights comes in gray. The news is war-ridden, shots never sounding as loud or as close as what we see in a movie, but childish, a popgun sound. We don't know what we see,

men or boys running holding guns, women hiding in doorways, making themselves thin, as if waiting out the rain.

Ma Mère is back in the hospital on a gurney in the hallway, getting brushed by people passing in thick-armed coats,
scarf ends tossed in her face, packages set down beside her by
people tired of carrying them who don't know she's there. Ma
Mère tries to sit up, she wants to see where she is, but her
robe's back slit has now moved to the front, exposing her pan-
tiless and scant-haired and folds so wrinkled and crumpled it
is hard to imagine there is an opening between them, a place
where this old woman was once young. And now others
notice her and widen their circle around her, not touching her
now as they walk past her, giving her room, looking at what
she is between her legs and then looking away, hoping staff
will wheel her back behind closed doors.

"Lie down," our mother says and our mother takes her big
black pocketbook and puts it over Ma Mère so no one can see
her exposed and she pushes down on Ma Mère's shoulders.

"Are you in pain?" the doctors ask her when they finally
have a room where they can see her.

"Oui, here," she says, she points to our mother's heavy
pocketbook still lying on top of her. The doctors hand our
mother back her pocketbook.

"That's much better. These are really good doctors," Ma
Mère says to our mother.

"And now do you feel pain?" the doctors ask her.

"Of course I feel pain, I am human," Ma Mère answers.

"No, this very moment," the doctors say.

"Well, my eyes, it's this light, you poor doctors, to have to work in this light. It's too bright. If I ran this hospital I would do something, I would turn down the lights," Ma Mère says.

"Yes, that would be nice," the doctors say.

"This is hurting me," Ma Mère says to our mother, and grabs our mother's arm so that she stands closer to her.

"What's hurting, ma cherie?" our mother says.

"My leg, of course, what else?" Ma Mère says.

The doctors have done more tests, they still can't operate they say, it's her blood, it's her brain, it's her heart, it's nothing to do with her leg. They say they are waiting for better conditions.

"You're not going sailing out on a stormy ocean, you're operating," our mother says. "Can't you just do it, this woman is in pain. She sleeps in a chair."

Ma Mère nods her head. "That's right, I sleep in a chair. My dreams are all straight-backed. Put your raincoats on, your rubber boots, men, let's operate," she says and she lays back and closes her eyes.

"No, no, no," the doctors say and we go home, wheeling Ma Mère out the main door and stealing the wheelchair. We go down the avenue and Ma Mère tries to grab the bumper of a bus. "Why keep pushing me?" she wants to know. "I'll just hold on."

John is disappearing. He is so thin now that his neck looks more like an arm poking up through his collar. I can see the shape of his skull under his hair.

"You're affecting business," I say. "Customers are afraid it's something the hot dogs do to you."

"What do you know?" John says.

"Your nose is bigger," I say. "Fuck," I say, "it's huge." John tries to poke me with his tongs.

"Get away," he says, his bony arm coming out from under his shirt cuff like a stick instead. He plays solitaire across the bin tops after lunch's rush, the cards humped from the steam of the cooking hot dogs below. John plays and points to the park. "It's like a heart," he says.

"The park, a heart?" I say.

"The people are the blood, they go in, they go out. Boom de boom de boom. Hear it?" he says. "Some blood stays in longer. Some blood goes out fast. It's a bad heart," he says.

* * *

New neighbors have moved in. A fat older woman and a younger skinny red-haired man. We try not to imagine them as lovers.

"It must be accord," our mother says. We can always hear the fat woman. Our house shakes when she walks across her floor. We can always smell the red-haired man. In the elevator going up or going down, we hold our hands to our noses. Our mother tells us red-haired people smell, they just do and she doesn't know why.

Their roaches become our roaches when they bomb. Even our cats are annoyed and flick angry tails when they try to sleep and the roaches climb their fur. We send their roaches back with our own bombs. This works for a week and then their roaches are bombed back to us, so many that there are albinos and ones with deformities, two heads and missing legs.

The fat woman welds. She works at night downtown somewhere on the docks. She wears her helmet with the plastic face shield home, saying more than once it has saved her life more than once. Gang boys with nunchucks have flown at her on late subway rides and they've thrown metal stars so hard they stuck into her plastic face shield and she had to pull them out with pliers. Our dog and cats attack her when she comes to our house. The cats hang from her clothes hissing and the dog nips at her rear. She comes through without knocking on our door. She comes and she sits down on our couch in her dirty coveralls and her mask and we stare at her shoes and wonder how she gets her feet into them and we wonder if the skinny red-haired man helps put her clothes on and is that what our mother means by their accord?

We show them the pipe where Jochen killed himself.

"Oh," they say, and then they are quiet.

They build a room around the area where the pipe is and use it for storage. We hear Jochen at night, we tell them. The fat woman says then she is glad she is down at the docks working at night. The skinny red-haired man says he doesn't hear, and that he sleeps with headphones on to keep out street noise.

Our mother has fainting spells now. "Oh, merde, it's just menopause," she says in the hallway, hitting the wall behind her so that when she falls she slides down the wall as if she were shot by a sniper across the way.

We try to pick her up. "Leave me here," she says. We all sit on the floor beside her. "Look, more hair," she says, and pulls it from her head and gives us each a handful.

"Thanks so much," we say. She puts her arms around us.

"My babies," she says, she brings us close to her. "Did I ever show you this?" she says. "It's Chinese. It calls the wild animals." She slaps a rhythm on the floor with her hands and her fists and shows us how it's done.

"Will it call our father?" Jody asks. Our mother stops her slapping.

"If we do it right," she says.

Our brother writes that they have been to consulates and embassies. They have passed through more sets of double doors than they ever have before. They have filled out reports in all the major cities. He has a callus on his finger from holding a pen. He writes our father's slut can give a perfect description of our father in Spanish, telling officials the color of his eyes, the number of brown stray hairs still remaining on his head, on the inside of his nose, but when it comes to ordering a cup of coffee or asking where the restroom is, their Spanish seems to leave them and they stumble over words, mixing English with the little they have learned.

Tourists sitting next to them on trains look at guidebooks, mapping out their trips, naming museums they will visit and sights they will see, but our brother and the slut sit and look through guidebooks trying to find hotels that are closest to the Guardia Civil, where they will spend their time filing reports.

The process is slow, he writes. There could be a long line out the double doors and into the street and when you get close you see there is only one person in the office behind a desk and just when you are about to be the next person called on, the person behind the desk opens his drawer and pulls out a handmade sign that's just a folded-over piece of paper. The sign in Spanish reads, "Out to lunch, be back in one hour," and the person puts the sign on his desk and gets up from his chair. And it's like watching the show *Mr. Rogers,* our brother writes, the person's movements are so slow as he goes to a hook on the wall and takes down his leather coat and puts his arms into the sleeves and walks slowly out the door and disappears. Then you have nothing left to do but hold your place in line and wait while the person behind the desk is down the street at some café, slowly chewing his food and taking small sips of his gaseous water with wine.

Our brother writes that one day the slut made a mistake, she walked into a church instead of the office of the Guardia Civil. He had to follow her in because she couldn't hear him calling to her, telling her it was the wrong place. He had the map, he tried to show her in the blue-green light coming in from the stained glass how she was wrong, but she kept walking forward, to the altar, as if expecting a desk and an office to appear.

Then only a few days later, our brother writes, he made a mistake himself. He took a wrong turn and they ended up at a public swimming pool. They entered the building anyway. He was curious to see Spanish girls in their swimsuits. The slut said you never know, your father might be here, and she walked forward, following the vapors of hot moist air and chlorine. She said maybe it was time they took matters into their own hands and started looking for him themselves instead of waiting for the authorities to find him.

It was the first time, he said, that the slut had made sense to him. His father was not going to be sitting on a hard bench at the Guardia Civil or the consulate waiting for them to come find him. He would be in bars, in restaurants, he would be enjoying himself. And then it sounded good, all of a sudden, our brother writes, to be in Spain. He looked around. There were girls everywhere with long hair and bright black shining eyes. Then the letters from our brother stop.

I can bend spoons. I learned it from a psychic on TV. I bend all that we have by just thinking about bending them. Our mother moves her chair away from me.

"Oh, merde, and you're my flesh and blood," she says.

"Bend this," Louisa says. She brings me the gun.

"I can only bend so much," I say, handing it back to her. I can bend things no more than the weight of spoons and sometimes keys. They hand me keys to our father's parents' house. The house he used to live in as a boy.

"These are useless," they say and hand me the keys and I hand them back bent and say they are more than useless now.

Our mother trips on books we have left on the floor and won't get up.

"I'm hurt," she says.

"Oh, sure," Louisa says. Our mother feels her pulse.

"I'm hardly here," she says. We start to tickle her, we close in by her neck, whisper whistling in her ears, our hair mixing with each others' and with what's left of hers. She is laughing, saying she can't breathe, saying yuck, her ears are wet with all our spit. She pinkie-fingers what she can, little jiggles back and forth in her canals.

"What's that you say? What's that you say? You've turned me deaf," she says. "My own children," she says.

The slut is shopping and thinking how the Spanish salesgirls are dying to rip off her clothes and dress her in new ones.

"No, gracias," she keeps on saying when they hold the clothes up to her neck, the tops of hanger hooks poking the soft place underneath her chin. The clothes they come at her with are all too young. Short black leather skirts and jerseys with stitched flowers and English words sewn on, words like Energy and Girl and Toxic and Rainbow.

The girls' dark long hair all smells of flowers and oils and their hair streams down the slut's shirtfront as they work around her, fastening buttons and clasps, and when the slut looks in the mirror it looks like her own hair and she touches it and tosses it behind her shoulder. The girls stand back exclaiming when they're done.

"Qué mono, de verdad," they say.

Mono she knows means monkey. "I am a monkey, really, that's what they're saying to me," she thinks. She takes the clothes off.

The girls bring the clothes to the counter, start to ring them up. The slut pulls out her wallet with the photos of Cal.

"Have you seen him?" she says.

"Su marido? Qué guapo!" they say. They look at the crystal

set on the table in the photo and call the other girls over so they can all look at how lovely it is.

"No, not my husband," the slut says. "Have you seen him?" she says again. The long-haired girls nod their heads and smile and take her credit card from her and charge her account and fold up her new clothes and put them in bags with more words on them. Words like Kick and Hot, written in bold slants on pink-colored see-through plastic.

Our brother waits outside on a bench looking at a map of the town. He keeps turning the map in a circle one way, and then the other way, trying to find where they are.

"How do you feel about a brother or sister?" the slut says.

"I've found the church, but which one," our brother says, still at the map his finger on an icon with a steeple.

"I thought it was early menopause, but it's not, I can feel kicks and bold punches," she says.

"No, it's menopause," our brother says. "You haven't seen my father for months," he says. He starts to circle places with a pen, the consulate and passport offices and banks to change money.

"I'm too tired," she says, when our brother wants to head first for the bank to ask if our father's been there for transactions. They sit and eat lunch by the water instead, ordering garlic soup and rabbit with mayonnaise. The old stooped-over waiter explained to them what conejo meant on the menu by holding up his liver-spotted hands like paws and taking hops across the patio. He hopped all the way down the street and back and then stopped at their table again and bent over and waved his hand behind him like a wiggling tail.

"How do you say, 'Whatever they pay you they don't pay you enough?'" our brother wants to know, so he can say it to the waiter.

"Just say 'energy,'" the slut says, "or 'toxic.' It means something here," she says.

They stop on a bridge and look out over a fast-running muddy-colored river. They read in a guidebook that the bad smell in the air comes from a paper plant.

"Would you be here if you could be not here?" our brother asks the slut.

"Isn't this the south?" she says.

"There's the south and there's the south and this is one south where no one wants to be," our brother says and so they rent a car and drive over winding roads, passing walls where cars have lost control, breaking through and smashing down below. The slut holds our brother's arm in fear the whole time that he drives.

"Let go," he says. "I can hardly steer."

"Stop the car," she says.

"Here?" our brother says.

"We've got to look over the edge, check if we can see him in a crashed-up car below."

"Oh, no," our brother says, "we're not even sure he's here in Spain, we're not going to start imagining him here in unimaginable accidents on top of it all."

"You could be the godfather," the slut says.

"I'd be the brother already," our brother says.

"Perhaps it's a boy, you could teach him what you know," the slut says.

"And what would that be?" our brother says.

"Teach him not to learn what you never bothered to learn," the slut says.

It's morning gym and dodgeballs have been let loose from the cinched necks of canvas bags and they bounce in all directions on the dusty gym floor.

"Go get them, girls," Miss Turd calls and then she whistles her whistle because we girls aren't making moves to pick them up and instead we are listening to them bouncing, their sounds hitting the ground getting weaker until finally they are at a roll and then a standstill.

"Girls!" Miss Turd yells and we still don't start picking them up until she starts naming names, telling who to pick up what ball. The boys are up above. They are running on a track that is creaking with their footsteps. Occasionally they stop and lean their red faces over, looking at us girls, shaking their hot heads all over us. Sweat showers down on us, slicking up the gym floor. Miss Turd is yelling for Mr. Caravello.

"Mr. Caravello, get those boys away from the rail. Off the rail!" she says from down below to the boys and she points at them saying, "You, with the T-shirt, off the rail," but they are all wearing T-shirts and the boys laugh and Miss Turd starts to make her way up the stairs, but the boys start running again, joining a pack where Miss Turd will never know which boy was the boy she wanted. Down below the Puerto Rican girls are trying to sit on the balls instead of the dirty gym floor they are disgusted to touch. It's not working, and they keep rolling off and laughing and Miss Turd sees them trying to sit on the balls and she comes running at them, yelling, "The air, all the air will go, get off, get off," she yells. "The air, my God!"

In the locker we are all Miss Turd. We are all screaming, "The air, my God, the air." Later, in lab, partners whisper to each other over split-open frogs, "The air, my God, the air." Slides of crucifixions are shown in art appreciation, the teacher tightening the lens on Jesus's thrown-back head, his mouth agape, the girls in our class giggling and filling in Jesus's words: "The air, my God, the air."

John's face is all red. He says it happened on the walk back home with his cart. Some boys took his money and then stuck his head into one of the hot dog bins filled with hot water.

"Even my ears are burnt," he says. He has put some kind of salve on the tips and lobes and curled-up creased places that glisten with yellow globs like axle grease.

"I'll find them for you," I say. "What did they look like?"

"Like fish," he says. "I saw them when my head was underwater."

"I'll tell the cop," I say. I walk into the park to find my stallion, who is swishing his tail by the jungle gym.

"Excuse me, sir," I say, but the cop doesn't look down at me and instead he urges the stallion forward and they walk out of the park.

"Excuse me!" I say louder, and only the stallion turns his head around to look at me, his bending neck rippling with wrinkled chestnut glossy hide.

"I need more," I tell John. "Their clothes, the way they wore their hair. Do you remember?"

"I thought about my ears when I was under," John says, "I thought, shit, I bet they'll burn and curl up like pork rinds."

"Is that all? Did you catch any names?"

"No," he says and then he says, "What about my eyes? Are they all right?"

John sits down on his milk crate. I think he's going to ask me to sit on his lap, but he doesn't, he just looks up and says, "Come fishing with me, would you?"

We go fishing. He brings a pack of hot dogs for bait and a fold-up rod he keeps next to the Hersheys in the bottom bin of his cart. We sit at the end of the pier. We don't catch anything, but all our bait gets eaten. We leave and on the way back John says, "I fed the whole goddamned fish population of the Hudson."

We are hungry all the time. We chop up onion and eat it between sliced bread spread with mayonnaise. Jody makes pancakes with just flour and water and fills them with sugar because we have no syrup. She pours grated cheese into a bowl and adds milk and stirs and holds the bowl up with both hands and swallows it like hot soup, too shallow for the dipping of a spoon. Our mother pulls at the fat of her belly.

"If I could slice this off and feed it to you, I would," she says. "Oh, your fucking, fucking father," she says. "Is there any word? There is no word, of course not," she says.

She shows us her hairbrush.

"It's not getting any better," she says and she throws the matted hairbrushed hair in balls on the floor where the cats take chase and bite the hair but stop to lick and lick and pull with their paws to get our mother's hair loose from their teeth.

"Hah," our mother says, taking a drink of her drink, "I could watch you cats all day."

There is no more Wood. We are in Metal this year. Our Metal teacher is young. His smock is gray like metal and there is metal on him too. A thin metal pen and pencil protector he fashioned and uses in his shirt front pocket. We call him Mr. Metal. When our sheets of metal are pushed through the table saw, filings fly through the air and the room begins to smell of the hot cut sheet metal. Our teacher is covered in the little filings that sparkle his clothes and his hair and everywhere on his face where his goggles weren't. We've seen metal on his tongue and his teeth. On stormy days when the sky outside our classroom windows is almost black, he glows with all his metal shining.

In the morning we stand where we are supposed to stand

at our workbenches. Mr. Metal waves a sparkly hand to us. When he tells us our project is to make boxes, I tell him I have a box already from wood, and what do I need a box for anyway? Mr. Metal answers that he doesn't give a goddamn what I use the box for, I could throw the box right out the friggin' window when I'm finished for all he cares.

"Yeah," the others say, "we don't care what you use the box for, just shut up," they tell me.

I get to work on my box. I make it bigger than I have to. I get the fat woman next door to help me. I build a box with a secret drawer in the back and weld things from the house onto the top. The tag for the dog's collar and a buffalo penny and some mind-bent spoons and some knobs from our drawers and my mother's wedding ring, which I find wedged in between the boards in the wall. I weld that in the secret drawer within the box. The fat woman helps me weld in her loft and sometimes I think I feel Jochen's breath by my neck, but it's probably just all the hot air from the torch the fat woman wields.

Rena glues her box with all her shells so that there is no metal left bare and the box could be made out of wood or metal and who would know. She is sending it to her father.

One night, when our mother's working late, my sisters and I decide to take turns being Ma Mère.

"Let me tell you about your father," Louisa says, sitting in a chair with a bathrobe belt we've tied around her so she really does look like Ma Mère, who is sitting next to us, sleeping in her chair while we play our game.

"When you were a baby," Louisa says, pointing to Jody, "He hugged you so hard that your eyes popped out of your head and rolled on the floor." We all laugh and then Louisa points to me. "When you were a baby he hugged you so hard he crushed your bones and turned them into mush."

Next it's Jody's turn. We unwrap the belt from Louisa and tie it around her.

"You, ma cherie," Jody says, doing Ma Mère's accent and pointing a crooked finger at me. "When you were a baby your father kissed you so many times you drowned in his saliva, you had to be rushed to the emergency room and, voilà! You were declared brain-dead for weeks! And you, ma cherie," she says to Louisa, "your father threw himself in front of a train for you, and now he's as thin as a piece of cardboard and disappears if he's standing sideways."

When it's my turn to have the belt tied around me, I can't think of what to say. I sit thinking for a moment and Louisa says, "She really is Ma Mère, she's falling asleep."

All that comes to me are things that already happened.

"I remember," I say, "how he once lost his hammer. He couldn't find it anywhere. He screamed at us to help him look for it. We searched a long time, then we noticed it was in his back pocket. We were afraid to tell him." And Louisa and Jody nod, remembering that too. "I remember," I say, "how he used to draw Mickey Mouse for us."

Louisa gets up and unties the belt from around me. "I

think I'd rather listen to Ma Mère than you," she says.

"Me too," Jody says. Then Ma Mère wakes up and looks down at herself where one of her belts is missing from her chest and she wants to know who stole it from her, who is it that will just let an old woman flop down to the floor and sit there in a pile of wrinkles and bones?

Our father has a sister we have never seen. Her name is Lydia and she lives in California. Every Christmas she sends boxes that smell of hickory and beneath the cellophane grass are smoky links of sausage and soft cheese in glass jars and bonuses of small cheap butter knives.

"This is what we get," our mother says, ripping open the plastic on a smoked sausage with her teeth and dipping it into the cheese, "because they're not blood. Poor adopted Lydia, she's lucky though, not to be related to her brother."

I can mind-bend the flowered butter knife in half so that it breaks in two. "You're really getting good at that," our mother says, pointing with her sausage at my bent knife.

Maybe Lydia knows where he is, we start thinking. "Let's call her," I say. We brush away the cellophane grass, searching for the sunny address in L.A. The ringing phone we picture on a bright countertop next to bowls of ripe green avocados and a Mexican maid named Guadeloupe who is busy on her knees, her cross around her neck swinging back and forth on a chain with every arthritic movement of her well-worn scrubbing hand. Lydia in the garden. Birds of Paradise surrounding her as she sits in her painted white ironwork fan-backed chair, bringing to her lips a glass of fruity coolness, the sky a perfect blue above.

"Oh, Lydia," our mother says, "you'll never guess who."

Lydia knows.

"Incredible," our mother says. "After all these years," she says. Our Aunt Lydia hasn't heard from our father, not since a year ago when he called and begged to borrow money and she lent it to him.

Our mother comes home giggling. There's a man from her office named Bob and she's dating him and she's going to leave us alone for two nights while she goes away with him for the weekend. We ask where she's going, we picture New England, a wraparound porch with rockers rocking in the wind and the name of the B & B hand-painted on wood that hangs from a post, but it's New Jersey, Newark, not far from his house, in a motel with curtains backed with foam as thick as rugs to keep out car lights from the nearby highway. We have a fear of New Jersey, we tell her, and she's the one who gave it us.

"Not Jersey," we say, "all the fires," we say. She holds her hand to her mouth, she cannot stop giggling.

"Leave us the number," we say. "Who knows what will happen while you're away? Call us every day." We look for her from the pier, sitting on the hood of Manolo's car, leaning back against the windshield. We use binoculars and look for fires. We find smoke.

"Those could be the small beginnings of great fires or just what's put out from smokestacks along the river," Louisa says.

Manolo opens the car door and comes out stretching and yawning. In his waistband is a small bottle of scotch, which he pulls out and drinks and holds up in a toast out toward the water, saying, "To your mother, may she fuck her brains out."

"How sweet," Louisa says, and she lifts up her foot and kicks at Manolo's bottle so that it falls and skates across the pier.

"Ah, carai," Manolo says. "You remind me of a woman I was once in love with," he tells Louisa.

"Tell me, did she look like this," Louisa says and with her hand outlines in the cold air a curvy shape.

"Sí, sí, Maria was her name. She had a beauty mark, right here and here," and Manolo points to places on his chest.

"They're called nipples," Louisa says.

Manolo laughs. "You girls know everything, don't you? Well, she had nipples and she had the beauty marks too. I called her 'cuatro pechos,' four breasts, you know," he says. He shakes his head and smiles, remembering.

She touches the foam-backed curtains, sees that they've been burned with cigarette holes. Bob has gone for ice, she can hear him filling the bucket down the hall. Car lights still make their way in where the curtains don't quite meet the window frame. A circle of light shines on the wall, as if a home movie were about to be shown, but the lens isn't focused yet. What is the film? she thinks. Is it of the Christmas where they drew the tree on the wall instead of buying one? Cal nailing small nails into the wall where he strung the lights and hung the decorations. One of the girls, she can't remember who, touching the drawn bows on the drawn presents on the wall, trying to pull one of the ends, unwrap a gift that someday would be whitewashed away. From the street, through the window, it looked real, and they preferred looking at it from outside. She went out with Cal after the children were in bed. They stood side by side and she reached out to hold his arm in hers, and he lifted up his arm and she thought he was doing it to put his arm around her shoulders, to bring her close, but he was doing it to point, he was looking at lights from planes in the sky, marveling at how close two came to crashing, and when they didn't, he was disappointed.

"Wouldn't that have been something?" he said to her, "if those two planes had wrecked above us?" And she had thought they already had, she was sure any moment they would see suitcases falling, opening as they fell through the sky, folded clothing and toothbrushes raining down.

They went back inside and Cal turned off the Christmas tree lights and she tucked blankets up around her sleeping children's chins and knocked twice for luck, lightly, on a wooden desk.

Bob wears glasses and says he is lucky he does because the ice machine shoots ice chips. The ice has left frosty shavings on his pants, at his zipper, where they melt and spread across as if the stain had come from him, as if he had, she thinks, and hopes, already done something without her back behind the ice machine in the dark corner of the hotel lobby. That over, now they could just have their drinks, sit across from each other in the room, watch the headlights from the cars pass over each others' faces and then return again to darkness. But Bob comes close to her. Standing, he holds her hand and it's cold and she pulls away and he says, "Sorry, it's from the ice."

He takes his glasses off and puts them folded on top of the television. They are so heavy, the frames and the lens both so thick, and she wants to tell him to put them back on, because how can he see without them? To him she must now appear as a blur. He wants to kiss her, she knows. She goes into the bathroom with her drink, saying she'll be right out. In the bathroom she looks at herself, at her bloodshot eyes, the small veins like red scattered roads and branching streams.

She runs the water so that he'll think she's washing her hands, but what she does is swallow her drink in gulps. When she comes out of the bathroom Bob is on the bed, his glasses still off, and he is patting the bed, asking why she doesn't come and lie down next to him. She goes to the foam-backed curtain, tries to draw it closed closer to the wall to keep out the car lights, but the curtain won't move. She goes behind the curtain, stands in front of the window, her hands on the cold glass looking out at the oncoming cars, and then she feels Bob behind her, he is reaching around her with the curtain still between them, through the foam she can softly feel what must be his hands moving over her breasts, trying to cup them and squeeze them, and then he is pressing her up against the glass, her face now turned to the side and he is lifting up the curtain and lifting up her skirt and pulling down her hose and her panties and she thinks it's all right, she can do this. Her eyes open, she looks down at the cars, thinks what the drivers must see, some woman's cheek pressed against glass, her hands pushing against the glass for balance, her hose around her ankles, the curtain moving back and forth behind her as if strange shapes were struggling, trying to find a way out, a way to breathe.

"I'd like to go out," Ma Mère says.

"You can't," our mother says.

"Isn't there a party? I hear music," she says.

"That's from downstairs, a movie is showing," our mother says.

Ma Mère dances sitting down, her arms lifting as if partners would come by and take her by the fingertips. She closes her eyes and moves her head back and forth to the movie music. She opens her eyes, "Remember your father?" she says to our mother. Our mother's cigarette glows brightly as we hear her suck her breath on it.

"Yes," our mother says, her exhaled smoke a spiral fading upward to the far corners of our skylight.

"He never gave me one," Ma Mère says.

"What's that, ma cherie?" our mother says.

"Oh, you know, you know," Ma Mère says, "One of those. I never had one with him. He never gave me one," she says.

"Mami, the children are here," our mother says.

"I know, but they are such old children now. They stink,

187

you know, the older ones, the smell of onion coming out from underneath their fat arms," Ma Mère says.

"Enough," our mother says.

"Your father would sew their mouths shut, if he saw them, so they could not eat. You realize that, don't you?" Ma Mère says to our mother.

"Papa would have done a lot of things I don't do," our mother says. "He might have cut your leg off, to keep you from the pain," our mother adds.

Ma Mère nods her head. "Oh, yes, the bastard would have done that without a moment's hesitation. Oh, ma cherie," Ma Mère says to our mother, "I'm better off to keep the leg, I'd like to be buried in my silk saffron-colored pants. Do you know the ones I mean?" Our mother says she does. We all remember the silk saffron-colored pants. She called them her pants to land planes, they were so bright. She's had them for years and wore them once when we all tumbled out of the car at some frozen lake upstate and tried lacing broken-laced ice skates onto our feet, feeding knotted worn laces through paint-chipped eyelets, while we sweated underneath our raspy nylon coats.

She was on the ice before any of us, gliding in her pants, singing songs in French and still smoking her cigarette. We could hear how well she skated before we even saw, the blades clean and slicing through snow-covered ice, more like the sound of knives being sharpened. Her tapered legs awhirl in spin. Chips of ice like stars shooting up around her while she went, clinging to the bottoms of the saffron-colored silk. We clapped when she was done, the snow falling from our mittens in flakes with the dull claps echoing against walls of the stone bridge we stood under.

"Bring me that," she says and we drag over the suitcase she brought when she first came to stay with us. Some of Bambi's black and white hairs are still matted on the plaid. She pulls the silk saffron-colored pants out and they smell of cigarette smoke and she hands them to me and tells me to wear them until she dies, she wants the pants to go places she can't go.

"To school?" I say.

"Sure, comme non?" she says, and then she says, "But make special efforts, wear them to other places too, elegant parties, uptown galleries and overseas."

"Overseas?" I say.

"Be careful on the tarmac, though," she says. "You may land a plane."

John sees me in the pants and turns me around, looking for the knob so he can turn their brightness down. He is trying to take out a tooth, sticking his fingers in the back of his mouth. He is losing another one and he says he'd rather take it out than wait for it to fall out just as he swallows a meal. No one buys a hot dog from him. "John, stop," I say.

"I can't," he says.

"Really," I say.

"Those pants have done a swell number on you," he says. "Where's the girl I went fishing with? Where's the girl in blue jeans?" he says and as he does his tooth comes loose and he pulls it out along with a sticky string of red saliva.

"You'll lose your corner," I say. "You'll have to fold up

your umbrella, let the others have a try, maybe they won't be pulling their teeth out in front of customers."

"Go away from me," John says. "Go on," he says and takes the mustard server, a metal lid with a metal rod attached that he dips into a cylinder filled with mustard, and with his outstretched arm he lunges towards me, the end of it dripping yellow mustard and he starts to splash it at me, the blobby drops falling to the sidewalk. I have to jump back, cover what I can of my pants so they don't stain, but John keeps coming at me and so I have to turn and run away from him.

We call the police station, just to see if there's been any news, but we can't get through to anyone who knows about our father's case.

A woman answers and Louisa tells her who we are and the woman asks, "Are you the kids who were in that basement fire?"

"No," Louisa says.

"I know," she says, "you're the ones who blew up the dumpster."

"No," Louisa says. "We're the kids with the missing father."

"Oh," she says and then she puts Louisa on hold and never picks up again.

Rena says the pants would get me pregnant in PR.

"Too tight, baby," she says. She says the way to be attractive is to do it so that no one else knows it but yourself. For instance, she says, wear a long skirt, but don't wear underwear.

"I'm not wearing any now," she says.

"You're not?" I say. I can't imagine walking down the city street, the grit from what my heels kick floating up between my legs, settling in crevices I'd later have to wipe, seeing the speckles of the city on my toilet tissue.

I take my box home from Metal and show it to my mother and she sees her wedding ring welded into it and she smiles.

"What a gift," she says, because she likes that she'll never again be able to slide the ring over her finger. She leaves it open on the table by her chair, dropping cigarette ashes into it when she thinks I'm not looking.

Bonnie's Hells Angel has been gone and now he flies in from Latvia. There his mother tried wiping off his tattoos in his sleep with a mixture of lye, lemons, and black dirt. She made him wear his father's pants, tied around his waist with a rope taken from the donkey's neck. The leather pants he arrived in she cut and made into drawstring purses for the ladies she met with at four every day. The donkey they now kicked to go forward instead of pulling it by the rope.

"Oh, what my mother could do with those pants," the Hells Angel says when he sees me in mine.

His swollen tattooed arm, he says, can go no higher than this, and he raises it to Bonnie's breast and holds it there.

"Thank God that's all she did to you," Bonnie says.

"No, that's not everything," the Hells Angel says and he shows us his underwear, pulling it out from his pants so we can read his name sewed there, Viktor. He says it wasn't just her, either, it was all those other four o'clock women too who sat in a circle, pitched in and sewed alongside his mother.

"Viktor? That's awful, that's really your name?" Bonnie says.

"Yes, Viktor," the Hells Angel says and Bonnie says that's the worst thing his mother could have done, letting her know his real name.

"Oh, baby," the Hells Angel says, "it's not so bad."

"Yes, it is. It really is," Bonnie says. "I need to be alone now," she says. The Hells Angel leaves, leaving his rope belt behind him which Bonnie holds up like a rat tail by one end and puts in the garbage.

The letters from Rena's father stop and when she writes to him, the letters come returned, the addressee unknown.

"Don't worry," I say, "after my brother finds our father, we'll send him to PR to find yours."

But it's Rena's father who finds her. In the middle of the night there's a knock at the door. Muy Hombre barks and it's Rena's father standing there with his suitcase in his hand and a bag made of fishnet holding oranges he said he picked himself, fighting rats who wanted to eat them first. The stems and leaves from the oranges poke out through the bag as if he had carried back from PR the whole tree and not just the fruit. Bonnie looks him over and she can't believe she once made love to the man.

"It wasn't just once," he reminds her, "it was countless

times and you screamed with pleasure like this," and then in the doorway he imitates for us the way Bonnie screamed while they made love and Bonnie grabs his arm and brings him into her place and tells him to be quiet, he'll wake the building.

He sleeps on the couch and then eventually he is sleeping every night with Bonnie and Rena says, "Listen, she is screaming again," and she is and Muy Hombre scratches at the door, wanting out, whining, the screams too loud for him. In the morning Rena's father cooks them breakfast and squeezes fresh orange juice, hanging the green leaves over the side of the glass and wedges on the side of the plates. Then he takes Bonnie's purse and finds her pills and flushes them down the toilet and when they float back up, he has to pull Bonnie out of the bathroom, her arm so far down the bowl her bathrobe sleeves are wet to the shoulder.

He tells Rena men in PR know when a woman does or does not wear underwear and men know the kind of women who do not wear it and he buys Rena packages of cotton underwear with flower buds all over them and tells her to wear them and Rena tells him they are not in PR. Rena's father wrestles Rena to the floor and pulls on the underwear over her legs. He tells her to wear them or he will glue them to her culo next time and Rena tells me I am lucky that my father is far away.

Rena's father tells me he knows I wear underwear, it's the pants that he's worried about. If I were his daughter he would hold me in a pickle barrel. "Let the brine fade the pants to something more pale, something more Sunday," he says.

Our brother writes the slut thinks she is getting bigger and she says it's high time she did something about it. In evening sunsets, she looks at her rounded silhouette against walls. They are looking for a doctor on a street in need of repair, in need of front doors on buildings, in need of beads on its curtains in its doorways, in need of lights beyond the beaded curtains, in need of inner voices, instead of the trickle of water from faucets, the creak of timber on a stair. The slut puts her ear to the wall, says she hears the sound of metal instruments placed on porcelain trays.

They find the entrance of the place and it looks like all the others, strings where the curtain beads once were threaded sway in the breeze as if just parted, as if someone had just come through or just gone out. The slut enters first, her shoe heels loud on the broken tiled floor.

"Hola! Hola!" she says. No one comes. Our brother sits in a folding chair, one of many, by the door.

"That's where the men wait," she says when she sees him sitting in the chair.

Our brother gets out of the chair and walks to the stairwell. "Hola," he says. A man comes down eating a peach. The man's hands are all wet with the juices.

"Are you the doctor?" the slut asks him in Spanish.

The man looks to the left of him and then to the right of him and then he says, "Yes, I am the doctor." The doctor leaves the peach on the desk and wipes his hand on a handkerchief.

"Where should I change?" the slut asks and the doctor points up to the ceiling. "Up the stairs?" the slut asks and the doctor nods. Our brother waits in one of the chairs where the men wait. When the doctor comes back down he reaches outside the doorway and rolls a metal gate down.

"Siesta," the doctor says. When the slut comes down the stairs she is holding her belly and trying to work the back of her shoe onto her heel.

"There was nothing there," the doctor says to our brother.

"Excuse me?" our brother says.

"No baby," the doctor says.

"I didn't think so," our brother says. The doctor nods his head. There is the bill, anyway, written out on lined paper from a small pad with pictures of fluffy cats on the cover which the doctor doesn't bother to rip off the page, but simply holds up the pad to show our brother the amount. To leave the place, the doctor lifts up the gate halfway, and the slut and our brother have to bend over and walk under it.

"I'm bleeding," the slut says as they walk down the street.

Our brother nods his head.

"Maybe the doctor lies," she says.

"What for?" our brother asks.

"To save the girls from guilt," the slut says.

There is a lead. A man in a bar has seen a man who might be our father.

"A man who looks Americano because of the shirts he wears," the man says.

Our brother and the slut sit at the bar every night. It is in a town by the sea and they hear the waves and feel a wind off the water while they sit on their stools. On the bar's patio, the wind cools them and blows through their hair and they order many drinks.

There are a lot of Americanos who come to the bar, and the slut sometimes says, "I almost thought that was him," and she'll point and our brother will see a man who he thinks must be from Texas by his boots and his hat and he'll say, "Him?" to the slut and she'll say, "His jaw, just his jaw."

They walk to their hotel late at night on the slick cobblestone streets, past castle ruins with glassless windows framing mountains and the moon. The slut holds her belly.

"That doctor left some inside me," she says. "Maybe an arm or a leg. A heel," she says. At the door to their rooms our brother wishes her goodnight and she takes his hand and puts it on her.

"Feel the kicks?" she says and our brother shakes his head and goes into his room.

When he thinks she's fallen asleep, he goes out again to a dance club, a place he doesn't expect to find our father, and watches all the Spanish girls in their short skirts and midriff tops moving in the flashing black lights and tries to catch their eyes.

At times he has told the slut he has given up hope for their father ever being in all of Spain and that he had better fly home. But the slut has grabbed onto his arm with her thin fingers cool through the madras shirt he has taken to wearing instead of the silk robe on days of record-breaking heat, and she begs him to stay, she can see her Cal on so many streets here, at so many bars, she is sure on days he is also swimming in the sea, breaststroking under the cloudless sky, his back red in the sun as he rises for his breaths, the water sliding off him leaving only the gleam of his burning skin.

Our mother shuts the window but the rickety frame is old, and large triangles of yellowed glass break loose from fractures in the pane and fall on her shoulders and clatter to the floor sounding like dinner plates come crashing down from shelves.

"Oh, Mom," we say. We tell her to come away from the window and she picks up glass shards and sails them out over our lot and the fat neighbor walks in and says, "That is exactly how they threw them at me." She means the Chinese stars the gang boys threw at her on the subway trains. Our mother walks to the garbage pile, sitting in one of the broken-legged chairs whose wicker seat is propped by a full plastic bag. Our mother sinks down. The fat neighbor stands sweaty under our hot skylight. The dog in the corner growls a low, constant growl at her. Our mother fluffs the garbage bags around her like pillows.

The fat neighbor says, "May I?" and takes a seat too on the pile of garbage where it really sinks down and compresses. The old greasy bags burst at the seams as she sits and garbage falls out—balled tin foil that once lined broiling pans, butter wrappers, and moth-ravaged sweaters.

The fat neighbor lifts our garbage up and tries to tuck it back into the bags, apologizing, and our mother nods her head. Then the fat neighbor asks for a glass of water and drinks it quickly and then goes to the wall and holds the glass up, listening to what she can hear on the other side, her loft. She says she swears he is having an affair. She has seen the other woman leaving their downstairs front door, and she has passed her in the hallway and has smelled him on the woman's long hair, has even seen, she says, red hair, the same as his, tangled in the woman's black.

"So?" our mother says and our mother snaps her fingers at us and we bring her a cigarette and she lights it and smokes.

The fat neighbor lowers her head and big tears fall down her face and would hit the floor, except that she's so fat and the tears hit her belly instead.

"Maybe I didn't mean 'so,'" our mother says. "Maybe I meant 'big deal,'" she says. "Or not 'big deal,' but 'merde.' Maybe I simply meant 'merde.'" Our mother keeps her cigarette between her lips and holds out her hands so that we lift her up and she can go to our fat neighbor and pat our fat neighbor on the back. Then our mother takes the glass from the fat neighbor's hand and she holds it up against the wall herself and listens. Our mother starts to laugh.

"What?" our fat neighbor says.

Our mother says it sounds like two men. Our mother asks if our fat neighbor is sure it isn't two men over there on the other side of the wall. Our fat neighbor shakes her head.

Our mother says it sounds like two old men to boot. Our mother laughs louder.

"Two old men huffing and wheezing and who can't figure out in which hole to put it," she says.

The neighbor starts out our door. We can still hear her crying.

"Merde," our mother says and wipes her eyes of her own tears from laughing. "Drop by any time," our mother yells to our neighbor who we can now hear walking in the hall, the light fixtures hanging from the ceiling shaking from the weight of her footsteps hitting the floor.

Our father is with us everywhere in the house. He stands in front of us like Manolo's outlined women. He is in front of Jody, I'm sure, in an orchard picking apples, giving her the reddest ones. He is in front of Louisa, too, the morning after a night of heavy rain, pointing to a grassy field covered in mushrooms. He is in front of our mother, or on our mother in the dark bed, the sweat on his head sparkling in street light coming in from a window, the phosphorescence of the bald.

He is in front of me, not drunk, not stumbling, but sitting in a chair, clearing his throat as if he will talk, ready to call my name, but he never does. Perhaps he brushes shoulders with Manolo's curvy women, or even Jochen's paint-stained fingers press upon his arm, steering him through the length of our house.

The silk saffron-colored pants have a hole in the seat. A small hole, but still, one that I worry will split wide open in Metal or English or Spanish. I stop wearing the pants and Ma Mère tells me it's about time, their bright color was starting to make her sick.

I sit across the street from John on the curb in the park. He waves me over and asks me where I've been. He shows me three Hersheys held fanned out like a poker hand and asks me to pick the one that I want. Nuts and no nuts and dark. I take all three with one hand, and stick them in the back of my jeans pocket.

"There's my girl," John says and he rubs his hand through my hair and he tells me he is going away. He is going back home on a plane to see if he can find his wife and children. He has saved enough one-dollar bills in ten cigar boxes that he plunked down at the travel agent's to pay for his ticket and his only regret is that he has not saved enough money to pay for new teeth and when he finds his wife she might only see an old man with a hole in his head.

"What about your children?" I say. "How will they know you?"

"They won't," he says.

Our mother is washed up and shiny, her face towel-rubbed and her elbows pumiced and her corns made smaller by single-edged razor blades she has sliced through the dead overgrown skin she has left in a pile on our floor where it gets stuck to feet bottoms and carried up at night under the covers of our beds.

She is going out. She doesn't know the man. A friend of hers has set it up. The friend has picked the spot. A restaurant brightly lit with waiters leaning over like whispering friends giving advice on what not to order.

"Merde," she says, she has smudged her eyeliner, the black under her eye now like a shadow of exhaustion. She licks her finger, tries to wipe it off, but the lower lid just becomes red and raised.

"I'm not going," she says.

"Come on," we say.

She has already read the subway map, figured out the number of stops she'll have to sit before she comes to the one by the restaurant.

"You want to go," we say and she says she does not and she throws the hairbrush at us and we hold up our hands to our faces and laugh so she throws more, whatever's beside her. Twisted empty packs of her cigarettes, the eyelash curler, bottles of witch hazel and Jean Naté cologne. We tell her she's beautiful and how great she looks and she says sure and don't you have homework to do?

"We don't have homework, but we do have work," I say. There is still the hunt for our father. We will go back to the precinct for any more news. It is raining and we rip holes for our heads in empty garbage bags and wear them outside and my sisters and I say we are all Poncho somebody. Poncho Villa, Poncho de Leon, Poncho and Judy.

The cops now say they have no clue, he could be in Africa for all they know.

"Oh, no, not Africa," we tell them, "the dingoes, the dirt, the flies carrying twelve different diseases, our father would never go there."

The cops smile, sit back in their chairs, invite us to hang our garbage bags on hooks in their hallway.

"You girls," they say, and shake their heads. When we leave we take our garbage bags off the hooks and they help us shimmy into them and make sure we know what bus to take home.

We dream of him and in the morning we tell each other our dreams where he is living with us again, fixing salads, whistling, standing in doorways. Our mother tells us there was a time before they thought to marry when he wrote her every day, long letters with a date and a time in the upper right corner, the hour always late and the pages sometimes stained purple by wine that had spilled as he lifted his glass and drank while he wrote.

"They were love letters of course," our mother says and she rolls her eyes and says, "Whoop de doo."

The letters are in boxes. Mice have nibbled the cardboard flaps and the corners of envelopes. Our mother says not to throw the letters out, they are all that's left of the love she'll never feel again.

"Boo hoo," she says and takes a drink of her drink.

Ma Mère has tried to pour wine straight from the bottle down her mouth, but she's missed, and there's a big red stain on the shoulder of her leopard-spotted robe so she now looks like a leopard who's been shot, poached, a dying breed finally finished off. We try to change her into a clean shirt, but what's easier is to change her into a garbage bag poncho instead and we ask her if she minds and she says she doesn't so we put one on her and call her Poncho Ma Mère.

Manolo comes over and kisses Poncho Ma Mère on the cheek and watches TV and takes a shower and we can hear him through our whole place singing. When he's out of the shower he goes through our mother's ashtrays looking for cigarette butts to smoke. He asks us how we all are and tells us that when he was a boy he worked in the olive fields and picked the olives in the high hot sun. He shows us his fingertips, still stained with oil.

"That's stain from cigarettes," Louisa says and Manolo reaches out and puts Louisa's hair behind her ears and asks her if she'll marry him.

"Of course," she says, "and where shall we honeymoon? Shall we push your broken car to face the Palisades instead? Will my ring be a lead seal from a bottle of wine?"

"Give me that gun," Manolo says, "that gun your brother had." He finds the gun and puts the barrel in his mouth and talks around the barrel, asking Louisa if this is what she wants.

"I can't understand you," Louisa says.

"Is this what you want?" he says again.

"You don't know how to use it? Is that what you're saying? I'll show you," Louisa says and she takes the gun from him and puts it in her own mouth and our mother walks in the door. Our mother doesn't scream, but runs so fast at Louisa that she knocks her over backward and grabs the gun from her. Then our mother throws the gun out the back window where we can't hear it land. We only hear the rain, which is falling loudly.

Still in her coat, our mother goes to Louisa and slaps her face and says, "Don't you ever do that again." Louisa's head doesn't even move after the force of our mother's slap. She just stares at our mother and then our mother slaps Manolo's face and Manolo says, "Do it again, I deserve it," and so our mother does. She slaps him again and then Jody and I back away from her, afraid she'll slap us next.

There were no bullets in the gun, but that doesn't matter

to our mother, she says no mother should have to come home to find her daughter's got a gun stuck in her mouth. Our mother pours herself a drink and lights a cigarette. She sits in her chair and rain from her coat drips to the floor. We turn on the TV for her, changing the channels, hoping for a war movie to calm her down.

The phone rings. Jody picks it up. "It's Dad," she says and we all look at the phone she holds out, as if we are to see his likeness in the earpiece, never wiped or washed, its shine dulled by our waxy ears, the buildup of our listening.

Our father explains to us the goddamn IRS, how they tried, the bastards, to get money from him he didn't have. How they squeezed and squeezed him and came to his door.

"Big thugs of men packing guns behind shiny blazers, odd colors for clothes—iguana and smoke. Connected men," he says, meant to scare him into paying his taxes.

"I left, cut out," he says, "and finished the film in Florida and lived at the racetrack walking hots. I slept in haylofts next to illegals who yelled out Spanish in their sleep. That's as close as I came to Spain," he says.

"I would have called," he says, "but the phone booth always had a line a mile long."

Our mother wants to call our brother, tell him to come home, we have found our father, but we don't have his number and it's later in Spain than where we are now, hours ahead. The slut sleeping, dreaming of snow and her brothers and the pageantry of Christmas. Our brother with a girl in a car at the top of a hill where down below the sea can't be seen through a milky-white mist. The condoms he's used he ties into knots, sends them sailing out the window and over where he thinks they will land on the water, but they just collect on a ledge, along with others other men have worn while with their girls in the back seats of cars. The girl is correcting him while he is inside her again.

"Mierda," she says and he says "mierda," but it is not the same as hers, and she says it again for him and their breaths fog the windows and her sliding stockinged foot on the window glass leaves a streak they can see the rising sun through.

The slut wakes and goes down to the sea, bruising her bare feet on rocks. The snack stands are rolled shut, their metal half doors down and flush with the countertops strewn with churros and chocolate sauce birds make a meal out of, flying off with the churros in their mouths like leafless branches from some kind of greasy holy tree. The slut starts to swim to an island. The island is just rock and when she gets there she cannot find footing to climb its slippery sides. She drags herself up, her knees turning bloody from small scrapes. She looks at the rest of Spain from her rock island. Small cars and mopeds are buzzing down the streets.

Then she sees Cal on shore, standing at a bar drinking coffee and reading the paper. She dives into the water and swims as fast as she can. She screams out Cal's name and swallows salt water and now all she can do is cough.

Still in her bathing suit she runs across the street, but just as she does, Cal walks to his car and drives off, taking a road that leads up to the mountains.

As the morning sun grows so strong her bare feet burn on the street she goes to her hotel to get our brother who is now sleeping. She knocks on his door, but he doesn't open it, so she opens it herself. She shakes his shoulder. She calls his name.

Our brother wakes up.

He can still smell the girl's perfume on his fingers and what may be the smell of her crotch, or his, he's not sure. He remembers the sunrise as a band of red seeping upward into the gray of the predawn and he remembers driving the girl home to her house in a alley where the sidewalk was rubble and the streetlights flickered off. His mother once said you should make a wish if you drive by and they turn on, but what do you do, he thought, when you drive by and they turn off and you are in Spain? Do you un-wish something?

The slut puts her hand on his arm, trying to pull him up, telling him she has found his father. Her fingers are still cool, like ivory on piano keys and they are that pale and he looks at her face, drawn and pale too, and he asks her what she's been doing all day.

"Here we are in Spain," he says, "by the water at the beach, and you look like you've been living in a cave. Where is your hairbrush?" he says. "Where are your clothes?"

There's a dark circle around her on the bed where she sits, her wet bathing suit soaking the sheets.

Our brother says mierda and the slut asks him to think of all the blood she lost from the baby and she asks him to think about the days she has spent going from door to door to door asking black-scarved gnarled old women if they have seen Cal.

Our brother at the wheel, they drive up the road the slut saw her Cal take. They pass through towns where they have to stop to let herds of goats cross the road, the slut holding her arm out the window, showing the herder the pictures of Cal and the herder shaking his head and the goats coming round to the driver's side, nibbling at our brother's sleeve.

"Keep the other fuckers off my corner." That's the job John has for me while he's away.

I lie on my back on the sidewalk's corner, my arms and legs spread-eagled, asking John if this is the way he wants it done.

"I don't know," he says. "Maybe they'll just wheel their carts over this curb and on top of you and crush you," he says. "Maybe there is no way."

"Have you flown?" he asks. "I came by boat."

"Never," I say.

"I wonder," he says, "if I'll be cold. I was cold on the boat," he says.

"I want to be an airborne Ranger, I want to fly the skies of danger," our father sings, he is closing the shades, turning the lights down low in his new place so no one from the street can see in. We are eating his pickled herring on Rye King crackers. Louisa is drawing faces of boys on paper napkins and

Jody is in the bathtub making bubbles with dish soap she has taken from the kitchen.

"In Spain?" our father says, and he starts to open a bottle of wine, "with your brother?"

"That's right," we tell him. He pours one glass of wine and drinks it down while still holding onto the bottle and then he pours himself another.

"What's her number?" he asks and we say we don't know and he says, "Mierda, isn't that what they say in Spain?" We don't answer. We lower our eyes, chewing our pickled herring on Rye King crackers.

"Isn't it mierda?" he yells in our faces. We nod our heads. I cough on my cracker that went down the wrong way. Louisa and Jody start to laugh behind closed mouths, their own cracker crumbs spewing forth. Our father stares at us and as he does we see the blood rushing to his head, his skin now the purple of the wine. We cannot stop laughing so we all run into the bathroom and sit on the tub.

We bend over, rocking ourselves. Tears come running down our faces. He talks to us through the closed door.

"I'm tired," he says. "Are you tired?" We don't say anything. We can hear him turn around and slide his back down the door so he is sitting on the floor now. We can hear him gulping at his wine.

"Why don't you go home," he says to us. We call our mother before we leave to tell her we're on our way.

"Don't forget money," she tells us. And so at the door, before we leave, we hold out our hands to our father and he laughs and in our hands he places lint from his pockets instead of money. "Jesus, Dad," we say, and let the lint sail back behind us.

"Tell your mother maybe next month. Tell your mother she'll just have to wait," our father says.

When we get home we tell our mother there is no money. She nods her head and takes a drink of her drink and wipes her mouth with the back of her hand.

She turns on the news to calm down and I see there's a bombing overseas and I swear I think I see John walking in circles in the middle of a road with his hands blown off. I imagine him back on the corner, his hands now hooks shaped like tongs custom-made to seize floating hot dogs from their bins.

"Let's go," Louisa says to me and Jody and so we leave and we're out on the street and it's a warmer night than we've had in a long time. We go to the park. Sit on the edge of the fountain, dangle our bare feet in the dark water. I can hear the clomp of hooves, my stallion patrolling the paths behind me. We look for change and find only pennies. We go to the pier, where Manolo's car sits parked, only it's rocking side to side and he's in it and the windows are steamy and there's the sound of the chassis squeaking as he moves inside with what must be one of the whores. We sit on the edge of the pier, saying we're thankful our feet don't reach the water from where we are, the river so dark who knows what would come swimming by and bite us. We go back home and play with the Ouija board but instead of moving across the printed letters, the pointer jumps to our laps, goes up our legs, our arms and breasts. All because we asked it who stole Louisa's bicycle from our hallway.

"This is a pervert spirit," Louisa says and she gets up from the game and goes to sit in her chair in front of the television, and the pointer jumps out from under our fingertips and moves across the floor towards her. We stand on our chairs and scream and the dog comes over and barks at the pointer and smashes down on it with her paw and then takes it in her mouth and thrashes her head back and forth. We throw the Ouija pointer and its board out the back window after the dog's chewed the plastic.

Our mother can't believe we threw the Ouija game out back. She says it'll lure spirits up from anywhere and everywhere, every Tom, Dick, and Harry spirit from other people's homes or passing by the avenue will now be drawn to where we live.

Our father is baking. We are at the oven window looking in, seeing through grease on the glass what our father calls his key lime pie. He bends close to us to look too and his smell comes at us strong. The oven's baking more than pie. The cotton of his striped shirt, his rolled back cuffs, the hairs at his arms, the patches of dried brown skin on his hands are cooking too. They smell of things between things—the legs spread wide, the spaces between travel-weary toes, the crease below our mother's breast that meets her rib, that is what our father smells like.

"Hotsy totsy newborn Nazi," our father says, admiring the loftiness of his meringue, its beaded sweating hollows and its curled tips.

We are at our mother's neck touching the wobbly moles, swearing there are more there than the last time we looked and also a hump there we haven't seen, a muscle, she says, so big and hard it could be the Hope Diamond. We poke and press it, telling her we want to know what it feels like. We tell her we want to know if we can see it sparkle through her skin and she bats her hands behind her head at ours and yells at us to stop.

It is her birthday and all she wants is P & Q and we ask her instead to name something we can wrap with paper and ribbon. We snip our scissors in the air and twirl our tape rolls on our fingers, holstered and ready for the duel. She drinks more on her birthday and smokes more and our place is red in the night with the exit light on in the hallway, the electric off again. We huddle by its glow singing her her birthday song in shorts, our legs crossed and red on the cool dusty wooden hallway floor.

"Oh, the dog, fuck," we say, we have forgotten to feed her because there is nothing to feed her. We call her over, our mother lets her lick her fingers from where she has dunked them in her drink. While our dog stands sideways to us we press our heads against her fur, roll ourselves against her ribs, hold her legs, listen to the workings of her hungry gut. We hang off her neck, admire her black wavy gumline, its ridges cupping foamy drool. Our mother cries and we lower our heads and Louisa says isn't it funny how little you can see in red light.

"Is that so?" the slut says, shielding midday sun with her hand looking at foothills our brother says is where the gypsies live in caves so shallow they must curl in their toes in the rains to keep them dry. The slut puts her hands on her hips, drums her fingers on her skirt embroidered with "Energy."

"Don't think we're going up there," our brother says.

"Yes, come on," she says and then they are off on foot, their sandaled feet slipping on the foothills' rubble, their tongues licking dry lips, their shirts stuck to the smalls of their backs with their sweat. By the time they reach a cave her skirt is dusted up, his ankle is sore from a twist along the rocky way, and the sun is beginning to slip down over the mountain's back. In the cave there is the smell of goat or sheep or ram or man, they do not know. Our brother wonders what's on the walls. He runs his palms over bumps and some kind of slime. Beneath their feet are green wine bottles, their labels gone.

"I'm going to be sick," she says and falls and our brother catches her and helps her to the floor of the cave where she closes her eyes and then falls asleep. Our brother looks out of the cave, out over the ocean, a blue the same blue as the sky. The slut stirs. Our brother looks back at her and thinks he can leave her. He will go back down to the car and drive north where he has heard the green hills are dotted with cows. He walks out of the cave but she hears him.

"You leave," she says, "and I will find you. I will certainly find you." He turns to her and smiles.

"I'm my father's son," he says, "and you can't find him." She brushes off her skirt as she stands and then she holds her hand out to him as if the cave were deeper and she could take him with her through dark passages. Our brother pats his shirt pocket.

"Have you got a cigarette?" he asks her. She shakes her head and he nods and then he walks toward her and takes her hand and then they are both down on the floor of the cave, their lovemaking sending the green bottles spinning and shoring up against the walls.

They find cigarettes at a bar at a blind curve in the road. They sit and drink beer and smoke and watch a skinny dog trot across the road and almost get hit by a car. The slut sees some of her brothers in our brother. The slitted nostrils and small ears, she says. Our brother calls to the dog and whistles, but it will not come and cars slam on their brakes and their tires screech and the burnt rubber smell fills the air. The cigarettes are French and stubby and the tobacco loosely packed and spilling from the ends and the slut asks if there is tobacco stuck to her lips. Our brother shakes his head but does not look at her.

"You should eat," our brother says and he orders her a

small sandwich, mostly bread with a thin slice of ham and butter. Our brother thinks again about the North and the cows dotting the green hills. The slut says she's cold, the sun is going down and they should go inside or get back in the car. The skinny dog is inside the bar now, circling stools where men with hats low on their heads sit and sip beer and drop shells from peanuts.

"I should go up north. The fish, I hear, is out of this world," our brother says. The slut shivers and rubs her upper arms.

"All right, then, we'll go north," she says. Our brother says he was thinking about going alone, how maybe she's right, that his father is still down south and she is sure to find him if she stays.

"Did I tell you about your father, how after every time he did it he thought he was having a heart attack?" she says and how at the hospital they listened to his heart and said it was gas, just gas and they gave him antacid. Our brother laughs, he can see our father afraid, his hand at his heart. The slut laughs too. "Yes, it was funny," she says.

Our brother leaves the slut while she's sleeping on the beach oiled in sun gel the color of carrots. The gel melting at her temples, magnifying the lines by her eyes. He goes for a coffee and drinks it while the waiter wipes his hands on his apron and sucks through his teeth, sounds for the pretty women walking by. Our brother, alone in the café, tries making the sounds himself, imagines himself with hair in the style of the waiter's hair, imagines the waiter after work on a motorbike riding high roads without railings overlooking the sea. The slut wakens to the man calling out, "Co-co-rico." He slices the coconuts on a splintered board he lays on the sand, the knife is curved as if for cutting cane. She wants the man to come to her. She waves hard, like a castaway who's just sighted a plane, her arm sweeping wide arcs in the air.

Our brother calls to tell us that he's fine. We can hear the rolling waves, we tell him, and he says it's just the roar of motorbikes. We can hear the slut's voice in the phone booth, we say, and he says it's passing Spanish girls. Our father's here, we tell him, come on home. We can hear him shaking his head, his hair now long rubbing against the earpiece, a faint sweeping noise.

"Well?" we say.

"All that time," he says, "and where was he?"

"You know," we say, "the IRS, the horses," we say. Can we hear our brother nod? He understands.

"Your gun is lost," Louisa says. "Come on home."

"Not yet," our brother says and he hangs up the phone. He walks back to the slut. The cocorico man is holding with two hands his knife like a scythe, bringing it down for a blow on the coconut that sends white shards flying up behind the slut's head as if it were her head the cocorico man had sliced open and the shards white matter from her brain.

"Señora, Señora," the cocorico man says, holding out the coconut sliced on the splintered board for her to take, a fanned display of its white meat held by the man's brown hand.

"There is the start of something here," she says, and reaches out and holds our brother's arm, puts it on her belly. And he feels it, he does, a small kick, a gentle jab, a pushing up from inside her. He lays his head on her, prepared to listen for it, aslosh in watery cradle.

After a moment he gets up and goes to the car. He drives alone, heading north, the call of co-co-rico fading, and green hills and the rolling haunch of cattle coming into view.

John is back.

"I never went," he says.

"You did, I saw you on the news," I say. "I swear."

"I took the bus," he says. "The bus stays on the ground. I passed marshlands. I saw them long-necked birds. I played some poker. I slept on the beach. You've never seen such washed-up crap. Those things, those pink plastic things women stick up them when they bleed. Those were all around me when I woke up. They looked like arms from plastic dolls. I lost my money. I was never lucky. Women touched me at the bar. I gave them chips so they wouldn't. Except one with gold on her lids. I gave her chips so she would."

"Your hand was cut off, I turned to every channel and you were there bleeding," I say.

"Oh, no, that wasn't me," he says. "I did get some fever from a sunburn, though. The woman with the gold above her eyes took care of me. She said she knew some shit about the sun." John loosens his white apron, lets the strings fly out behind him, the apron like a stingray swimming up from a sandy ocean bottom.

*　*　*

Ma Mère is hitting my leg, showing me where she has her pain.

"That hurts," I say.

"It really hurts more than that," she says. She bites her bottom lip. She rocks back and forth, her arms around her in a hug.

The phone rings.

It's our father down and out and jailed and using up his one-time call from Mobile, Alabama.

"Possession," he says.

"Pot?" Louisa says.

"Marygeewanna is what they call it here," he says. We have to bail him out and wire him two hundred dollars. He says he'll pay us back. We have to ask our mother for the cash.

"Let him rot in there," our mother says, "let them show him Southern hospitality. They'll feed him grits in the clinker, he'll be all right," she says. We cry. We break open Jody's piggy bank she keeps on the shelf by her mouse cage, and nothing's in there but some pennies and cedar shavings. Our mother hits herself, slaps her face. "I must be an idiot," she says and she signs over the paycheck she's just received so we can cash it at the E & B and set our father free.

There is no more Metal. We are scheduled with free time. Periods where we walk the streets, sit in the park, decorate the margins of our pages with clumpy ink from ballpoint pens and write our names on the sides of rubber soles. Rena sits on her boyfriend's lap, facing him, kissing him, braiding his long hair, holding the end above her lip. She turns to me so I can see her mustache and in her deepest voice calls out my name and says, "This is your father talking."

Later, after her boyfriend leaves, I say to Rena, "Fuck, Rena, all these boys. It's a little disgusting."

"Disgusting? Maybe what's disgusting is no boys. Who do you like, baby? Is it that hot dog man? Is he your lover?"

"Fuck, no," I say.

"Mr. Lenin, then?" she asks.

"Gross, no," I say.

"Then who, baby, who?" she asks.

I shake my head. All I can think of to tell her I like is some cop's horse. Some stallion. I don't even know his name. But I don't tell her anything. I don't have to. I know she knows there's no one. I wish there was. I wish there was some Ramón or Realidad.

Then Rena hugs me. I smell grape in her hair. Some shampoo or conditioner she used in the morning. It is a smell I think I can fall into. Fuck, why can't I be Rena? Boys and a father and grape in my hair? Rena stops hugging me.

"I know what you need, baby," she says. From her jeans pocket she pulls out a small box and lifts the lid. There are blue pills and black and pink.

"Take a blue. I had one earlier," she says.

"Christ, Rena," I say.

"Well, then try a black beauty, Bonnie always takes a

black beauty," she says.

"You're going to end up like your mother," I tell Rena.

"We all end up like our mothers," Rena says. "Baby, don't you know anything?"

I walk back to school.

Sharks are sliced and their innards cut and lifted and placed on slate tables in the labs. The halls smell like the ocean gone bad—rotten fish and stinking seaweed. I look in classroom door windows at teachers who once were mine. They wear the same sweaters, the same scuffed shoes I once made fun of. I miss those teachers, how they lowered their heads over my pages, tried to read my scrawl. I'd like to open a door, take the seat that once was mine, feel their heads close to me, the not so unpleasant smell of their just-finished lunch on their lips, a yeasty whiff of packaged bread coming from their mouths when they speak, their voices low and calm, the others at a problem in their books, the pages filled with the beauty of geometry. My pencil sharp, my circles perfect. The teacher ready with an answer.

I get home and sit next to Ma Mère and she starts to tell me again about our father. "When you were a baby he would walk you around the room for hours..." she begins, but then she stops. "You've heard this before," she says.

I nod my head.

"I've told you all I know," she says. "Your father, I've been thinking, maybe he wasn't such a good father after all."

I nod my head again.

"Your mother was right to leave him," she says.

Then I laugh, and Ma Mère laughs too, enjoying her own joke. Her eyes turning into slits, her cheek bones lifting high and wrinkles forming on her forehead like steps.

"You are getting older, aren't you?" she says after we've quieted down, after our laughter has stopped and the steps on her forehead have disappeared and all that's left are lines. She holds onto my chin and looks at my eyes.

"When you paint them you must try to make them look bigger," she says.

"Will I see more?" I say.

"You will always see less as you grow older," she says. "Otherwise you would not want to go on." She tells me to get one of my mother's makeup pencils and she licks the point and with a shaky hand she draws lines underneath my eyes.

"There," she says. I look in the mirror.

"I look surprised," I say, "a doe in the headlights."

"Men like that," she says.

"Are there deer in France?" I say.

"Oui," she says, "all over the streets."

Our brother is back. He has gifts for us from Spain, miniature bullfighters' capes we clip to our shoulders and fans carved from sandalwood he teaches us how to whip open and hold to our faces, fanning furiously in the way we believe señoras and señoritas do as they stand in the stands under a hot Spanish sun. Our brother looks different, his dark hair a little wavy, a little Spanish, we say. He wears gummy-soled shoes. When he walks through the house we cannot hear his footsteps and we startle when he comes upon us. We ask where he has put his blue silk fire-breathing dragon robe and he says he wore the robe so much the cloth at the shoulders became bare and his skin stuck out like epaulets on a uniform for no army known to man.

Maybe years later the slut has the look of a woman who has lived somewhere before. She now knows the words for certain things, is familiar with three-day winds, the roads of Morocco, the strongholds of the British, the uses of kohl, the laying and folding styles of napkins for all sorts of tables, has heard music from instruments deep-bellied and two-stringed, cries that were songs, waves washing on rock, coral, and sand. She has pens filled with ink and some that are plumed. Slippers sewn with gold thread and pointed toes. Gum smelling of leaves. Oil in wax-sealed jars. Says "no" as a question after her sentences. Pedals backward to brake on a bike that only brakes by hand. Eats steak with a knife like it was a fork. Looks skyward for the grace of God. Digs in a garden with shards of broken bowl. Calls dogs with the clap of her hands. Trims her nail with a blade. Twists her hair and burns the broken, frayed ends. Rubs her teeth with hollow grass blades in the morning and night. Wears skirts that are scarves knotted at the hip. Writes in a leather-bound book. Totes a cat on her shoulder. She has seen the torturous wonders of the Middle Age, has swung the creaky wooden door of the iron maiden, felt the pointed bloodstained tip of the anal pyramid, turned the rack's wheel that stretched the victims' limbs. Joins children at games on the street, throwing off her shoes and hiking up her dress, letting the girls try her perfume kept in a vial, applied with a stick to the small beating veins at their necks. She gives them names they have never heard before and tells them they are the words for tree, sky and lake in a country where the girls never bathe but are licked clean by cows.

She writes to a daughter she thinks she had. The letters never get mailed and even if she did know where to send them, she doesn't know she would. The daughter is perhaps where she left her, under the Damas sign on a door in a restaurant in Spain. That is how she sees her now, a cutout shape of a girl in a dress on the door to the toilets. The letters are statements, rushes of visions come to her while seated on buses, on plush movie-house chairs, benches spilled with pigeon crap.

"Yearning sounds like what it means," she writes. "Above it all is the underbelly of something else." "I can die." "Who has seen me ever juggle. Did you know I can?" The pen point scratching fast on onion paper, the plume dipping and rising like a grounded bird beating wings in attempted flight.

"Cut all vegetables by hand. The cook is in the pudding. Let the guests taste you. Oh, and about your menses. Get the moon to phase with you. The tide to lap at your door. Call it Rose or Aunty, but never what it is. If caught wearing white and you stain, stand and spread out your skirt, let the boys read into it shapes like blots of ink. Imagine the abdominal pain is forty times less painful than having a baby, no, imagine sixty times. Deliver blows with your fist and then curse, you are really bleeding now and nowhere near knowing. Shhh, listen to your hair getting longer, the turns it takes when growing in a curl."

Sometimes she twists the pages of the letters together and lights the ends on the oven's small pilot flame and throws the letters in the sink, watching them burn and then smoke when she douses them with water from the faucet. She likes to think the daughter eats sardines and sausage made with blood. The daughter was born bleeding, the midwife called it "primero sangre." The midwife called her Señora and the baby La Niña and the midwife was called Vieja, and so she said "Vieja, take her." She did not hold La Niña to her

233

breast and she tried to put her in Vieja's arms but Vieja shook her head and gathered up her bag and the cord she had already asked to keep for drying and grinding into powder for strength and she said, "No, no, no, señora," and backed out through the beaded curtain in the door while still shaking her head. Sore and still bleeding, she walked to the restaurant next door, carrying the baby who did not cry in her arms, and she walked up to beautifully dressed women eating, wanting to place the baby in their arms, wanting them to put down their forks, hold up their pretty hands and take her daughter from her. They did not even look at her as she walked through and she realized she must look like a gypsy come to beg, the baby's blanket falling and dragging to the floor, and her own hair matted to her forehead with the sweat of the labor. She left the baby in front of the door to the toilets where its arm came undone from the swaddling blanket and its hand waved in the air.

"Select milk from the back rows of cases, never the front, for that is what will spoil first. Learn to chop onion with your eyes closed. Brush your teeth in the shower. I think we were meant to. Watermelons once had seeds. The sun is not a star." She tears the letters into bits and lets them snow on heads of children who play below in the street. Cal still calls. He is drunk. He is asking for money, for fifty dollars, for anything she can spare because he has not eaten in a week. She is growing lumps behind her ears that move between her fingers and she finds herself feeling the lumps when she's in line at the grocery or when she's on the phone or trying to fall asleep at night. She has caught herself in the mirror while feeling these lumps and she looks like an old woman who cannot hear well and is cupping her ears, hoping to capture words that would otherwise float past.

I go to John and I sit on the curb by his cart. He sits down next to me and touches my hair, moving it away from my eyes so I can see and then he points, showing me two pigeons fighting in the gutter over a broken hot dog he has thrown them. He claps his hands together and laughs because the fight is a good one, the pigeons' beaks stuck together.

"It's to the death," he says and I stand up. I cannot watch for very long. "Where are you going?" John asks and I shrug and let my hair fall back in front of my eyes.

"How about some?" he says and he pulls out a Hershey from his apron pocket and pats his knees so I'll come to him and sit on his lap.

"No thank you," I say.

"No thank you, what's that? I never heard you say that before," he says. "Fuck, that is what you say. That is all you know how to say," he says.

"Fuck, no thank you," I say. He nods his head and keeps nodding it.

"Remember me, kid," he says.

"Why, where are you going?" I ask.

"It's you who's left, I'm not going anywhere," he says and he puts his Hershey back into his pocket.

"No," I say, "I won't remember you."

"Remember all the crap I gave you, the Hersheys and the sodas and the hot dogs," he says, "just remember that." He stands and puts his hands on the handles of his cart as if he's about to push it in front of him, but he doesn't go anywhere, he just stands, looking out at the park, and it is me who walks backward, away from him, watching him get smaller, deciding to see if I can walk all the way home backwards, knowing I'm getting closer because the bells from the church near my home are ringing and the sound is getting louder as I walk.

Our mother comes home dangling a set of keys. A few weeks at a lake cabin in the country. A woman at work is lending it to us. Our mother says the woman at work is moving up, now has other options and a chalet in the Alps for her vacation needs. The cabin, the woman warned, had not been summered in since summers long gone. She handed over the keys to our mother on a miniature gold stirrup key chain. "Yee haw," our mother said and says again as she turns the key in the front door's lock.

Inside mold grows in creeping fashion up the sparsely whitewashed walls. The cabin smells as it if has been sitting at the bottom of the lake for years and was just lifted up and set in the woods where we are, where the sun hardly shines, where its walls and peeling-down wallpaper and warped floorboards will never dry. The mold grows in corners up from the floor in fuzzy humped shapes like the backs of furry animals most likely found in these dark woods.

Where's the lake? We look out windows ridden with bullet holes from the guns of poorly aimed hunters or from BB guns town boys shot for winter fun. "The lake is near," our mother says, while looking out at the trees with leafy green tops and long grooves in the bark like furrows in a farmer's field. Our brother carries Ma Mère and puts her on a wrought-iron chair in the glassed-in porch where she and our mother drink Bloody Marys they stir with their fingers, flecks of black pepper swirling in a whirlpool of red. Our brother sits with them on the glassed-in porch and drinks with them, saying he has developed a taste for tomato in Spain. "I will will myself to die here in this cabin," Ma Mère says to our mother.

Branches press against the windows. Roots finger up through the crawl space beneath the cabin. We are dappled here. Triangles and circles of light play on our summer tees, our suntanned faces, our melting pops of lemon and of lime.

The dog cannot go out without coming back in having picked up something from outside in her fur. Foxtails in between her toes she worries with her muzzle and bits of twigs hang from her brushlike fanning tail.

They call them "bloodies," their drinks, and we leave Ma Mère and our mother and our brother drinking them and we go explore. Sticks in hand, we head for the lake swatting spider webs aside and following a path we are not sure is a path but could be just the space between rows where skunk cabbage grows and where we weave through slender maples just our height, our heads level with their modest show of leaves about to turn. We are coming on fall.

The lake is a mirror and the wind is at bay. We walk to the end of the dock, sidestepping dried dead worms pulled waterlogged from hooks that never felt a bite. We look down at ourselves in the smooth lake. Above our heads clouds float by and a raven caws and crosses the lake. Our eyes follow it. There's nothing over there we see, just more our-sized maple trees, and tufts of grass growing on a black and muddy shore. There's a boat by our dock half-filled with water and a split wooden oar and a life vest missing straps.

We jump into the boat and set to bailing. The dog on the dock starts to bark. We are breaking all her rules. Louisa paddles us away. The lake is clear. This is the water we drink, she says, this is the reservoir. We can see fish swim beneath us and turtles in an upward climb.

Later we say we taste it in the water from the tap, the wood from the split wooden oar. Taste, we say, and offer some to our mother, but she says, "No, thanks, I've got my bloody."

There is a family of eleven who shares our woods. At night in our beds we can hear them. A door slam, their cat, the mother running baths.

"Catholic," our mother says, shaking her head.

We see the mother reading aloud to them from a Bible while they are snapping beans at her feet and listening.

Sometimes we listen too, we cannot help it. The mother's voice is loud. It carries down to us on days we go to the lake and jump from rock to rock in the shallows.

"The Lord sayeth," we hear and a breeze ruffles the lake's water as if it were not a breeze at all, but the power of her words. The sun is warm on us while we sit on the rocks, each of us on a different one, our knees pulled to our chins. If someone from the hill looked down, he might not see the rocks, but only us, seeming to float on top of the water. But no one ever sees us. It is a quiet lake, except for the crow who caws and travels between the banks or the sound of our one oar splashing through the water in the sinking boat we sail.

Our mother says she does not want us listening to the mother of eleven read.

"Get religion from the lake," she tells us. She goes down with us sometimes. We hold her bloody for her while she negotiates paths and when she misses her step she grabs at maple leaves. She stops and stares and looks out at the water and breathes deeply and then motions for us to give her a drink of her bloody and then she puts her hand on her chest as if her heart were hurting her.

"This might be lovelier than France," she says and then she sits on the pier and lights a cigarette and cups her hand to hold the falling ash which she later drops on the path on the walk back up to the cabin in the woods.

Ma Mère looks out her glassed-in porch and points to a mockingbird in a tree branch.

"Whippoorwill, whippoorwill," she says in a French

accent and raps the porch glass. The bird turns his head to each side.

"Say it, merde," she says.

The family of eleven bakes bread and we smell it down our way, a sweet smell of something our mother thinks is molasses.

"I can bake," our mother says and she tries to light our oven but the blue flame explodes out the oven door and blackens the white enamel sides.

"How about I teach you French?" Ma Mère says and tells us to sit in a circle at her feet.

She says, "Repetez moi, whippoorwill, whippoorwill."

"That's not French," we say.

"Oh, merde," she says. "Just say it. Someone. Please," she says.

She is the first to spot our father in a car that sways from side to side as it makes its way up our driveway, humped and bumpy with piles of dirt made by rains and winter weather past. "Cherie," she calls to our mother, "your husband's come. He wants you to take him back."

Our father found out where we were when he called our mother's place of work. He looks different. He's hunched over, looking like he is trying to run away from an outstretched arm of the law through some low-ceilinged tunnel. We have the outstretched part right, his hand reaching for a handout, whatever we can spare. He is in debt up to his ears. Lucky, he says, to still be wearing the shirt on his back. Our mother won't come out. She sits with Ma Mère in the cabin with the door locked. He makes us walk by his car. Note the baldness of his tires, the needle of the gas gauge hovering at empty, the spiderweb crack in the windshield. Too bad, we say. We dig into our pockets for him. Up comes a popsicle stick, a joke printed on the blond wood. Hey Dad, what did the fish say when he hit the wall? Damn.

He doesn't like it. All the borrowing he has to do, he says, he has no choice, you see. It was the man at the betting window's fault who did not hear him correctly, who gave him the wrong ticket on a horse, otherwise he'd be sitting pretty right now. Our brother comes outside, his madras looking cool and summery, ample in the sleeves. He shakes our father's hand. "How's it going, Dad?" he says.

Our mother mouths to us from behind the porch window that our father must leave. Ma Mère makes a gesture, shooing him away with her hands, the tips of her fingers pointing down and pushing him away. We say we have to go. We have to get back inside the cabin. Dark is coming on. Mosquitoes buzz past our ears. We slap our arms and legs.

"Aren't we a family?" he says, but he is not looking at us when he says it, he is looking at his car. At the balding tires, shiny and smooth as innertubes. Then he stands by each one of us and hugs us, not from the front, but from the side. He takes turns with us, putting one arm across our shoulders, pulling us close to him. He stands that way for a moment with each one of us, as if there is someone taking our picture and he is making sure we stay still long enough so that the shot can be taken.

And then our brother says to us, let's go back inside. Out

through bullet holes in our cabin we watch our father leave, over the humpy, bumpy driveway, his car lumbering, sometimes scraping bottom, sending up the summer dust.

Ma Mère dies days later saying it herself. Her mouth slightly open, the "will" sound stuck in her throat that we swear we hear released when she's lifted from her chair and taken away by the ambulance. Our mother holds her hand, insists on it, has the coroner unzip the black bag slightly so she can slip her hand in there and hold onto Ma Mère as if Ma Mère were not altogether dead, just injured somehow and our mother was a comfort on the ride to the hospital.

Our mother and brother having left with the ambulance, my sisters and I head down to the lake. We can hear the mother of eleven. She is singing now, a song we can't quite make out, just a "Jesus" here and there.

It is night but the moon is bright and we climb in our sinking boat and push off from shore. In the middle of the lake we drift. The mother of eleven still sings. We bail for a while, then we tire and quit and let the water come above our chests. "We're going down," Louisa says and as she does our arms float from the sides of the boat and the boat comes away like a skirt we let fall from our hips. We tread water. The mother of eleven still sings. I say I'm diving down. Don't, they say, think of all the things down there. But I take a breath anyway and dive just to say I did. For a moment I can still hear the mother's song. But then there's only a swishing sound, all the fish going by, their tails and fins waving, the opening and closing of their gills, the eyes of the turtle slowly moving to and fro, the eel slipping past, the grazing barb of a catfish touching muddy bottom. Down deeper I go, to where I can hear only the beating of my heart and it sounds caged and angry, my ribs metal bars it can't squeeze between or saw through, and I wonder if it knows how close it is to breaking my bones and setting itself free.

When I come back up, my sisters are gone. They have swum to the other shore and are calling for me. I meet them there. We wring out our summer tees. Amazing, they say, the song of the mother of eleven sounding louder here, as if this is where she wanted her voice to reach.

The other shore is no different from our shore. The same skinny maples grow, the same skunk cabbage. Maybe this isn't the other shore. Maybe we are where we were all along, we think. We walk a little ways. Into the thick of trees. But then we stop. This is too scary, we think. The moonlight blocked by thick pine boughs and what if everything was the same on this side of the lake as on the other side? What if we walked and found the same cabin we were staying in, the same family of eleven, the same family of us? We turn and run back to the lake. We dive in and swim back to our shore. On the pier, we see someone standing. In the water we stop and clutch each other. Then we see who it is, we can tell by the pointed ears, and we call to her. She jumps in with a loud splash and we float on our backs, offer her a place to grab us by the collars of our summer tees and we let her do what she loves to do best, save us. One by one we are rescued, towed to our shore in the moonlight where our silver faces are licked back to life.

"Is this enough?" our mother says.

"Enough of what?" we ask.

"The lake, the cabin, all the fucking R & R," she says. We nod, our heads still wet, our hair still smelling of the lake. We are ready to go home.

Back in the city, we can taste it in the tap water, the sinking boat we sailed and let fall to the bottom of the lake. Louisa has done research. She has brushed up on her watersheds, knows where New York gets its crystal-clear supply. This is from there, she says, meaning the water she holds in a glass. We drink our water down and I think how what I'm tasting tastes like all of it, the fish, the turtles, the eels, the catfish, myself, my summer T, and the words that the mother of eleven sang that rippled on the surface.

School has started up again, so many weeks now our notebooks are old, the paper ripping from the spiral spines and the covers worn and thickly doodled.

Rena's father moved her family. He found a house in Queens where the carpets were plush and the squirrels in the neighborhood healthier looking than here, that was the deciding factor, he had said, their glossy fur.

We tell our mother that it's spring when it's supposed to come upon her, this wild urge to clean. The barrel with the dull-bladed ice skates and the old wax-stained sweaters is dropped in a box at Goodwill.

"That's a shame," she says, "that's what's wrong with this country. Spring is for flowers, not cleaning," she says.

"That's what's wrong with this country," she says it again the day I get my period. She has taken us all out to a restaurant to celebrate. People don't celebrate that kind of stuff, we tell her. "Oh, pooh," she says, "damn this country, anyway," and she orders me champagne. "To being a woman," she says.

"Here, here," my brother and my sisters say and I am given presents and kisses on my cheeks. Then our brother gets up and leaves. He has a job now, playing mandolin and guitar in an Irish band. He'll come home late. When we get home our mother sends the elevator down for him so he won't have to walk up the five flights of stairs with his instruments when he gets back. She opens up the door and pulls the cable inside the elevator, then she steps back and the elevator travels down in the dark by itself. But then our dog comes running through the hallway. Her eyes not so good now, maybe she thinks when she runs past our mother's legs and steps down into the air that the elevator is still there, that there's a possibility we will take her on a walk. But the elevator isn't there and our dog falls down the shaft. She hits the top of the elevator where there's a little trap door. She falls through the door and the elevator automatically stops between floors. We run downstairs and we hear her whimpering. We call her name.

We can't move the elevator and finally the fire department has to come. It isn't until morning that they are able to pull her out. She is stiff and dead, but the fur at her neck is still soft. We all feel it and say our goodbyes and then her fur becomes wet with our tears and our mother says "Merde" and I say "Fuck" and we all say how she was a good dog, the best dog. We have nowhere to bury her and so we find a huge cardboard box, a box for refrigerators that our neighbor had. We lift our dog into the box and leave her on the corner by a city wastebasket and we call the sanitation department and wait for them to come. When they come they put the box into the garbage truck and the back of it starts going around and around, and our dog in her refrigerator box starts to do circles in the truck and get smashed and made small.

There are a few more trips to where our father now lives alone in the country, but we don't let the visits last long. Maybe we are all afraid of the transfer effect, of us turning into him or him taking what is good inside us for himself. We leave. We stand on the steps of the train and look down to where he stands, noticing new blotches, the toll the summer sun has taken on his bald head, and we wonder if years later we will always have this bird's-eye view of him. As we grow taller will his shoulders stoop more with age, more with life? Will shapes of unknown lakes and oceans start appearing on his head as if we are seeing a satellite's photograph, the faraway image sent back to us here on Earth? When the time comes, will we carry him from his chair to his bed, from his bed to the grave? Will we stand by, mourners who have already mourned for him long ago when he was still alive? Done with our mourning, will what we notice on that day only be the hillside he is buried in, the wildflowers in bloom, the color of the sky that ordinary unlike any other day? Will we walk back arm-linked, my brother and sisters and I, down the grassy hillside, our legs falling into a stumbling run, a flying off almost to home? Our mother waiting there in her chair, drink topped off, and up her sleeve a gaming plan. Five-card draw, with peanut shells to serve as chips and cards held close to chests. We'll burn the hours, deny the night its darkening hold. What could ever hold us now? What would ever dare? Our bags of garbage are fortress walls, the lolling cats our lions barely tamed, the empty lot out back our moat of sorts. Our mother splays out her colored pairs, cackling, delighted with her win, spit dappling her kings and queens and the splintered table where we play. Beneath the wood, our knees together, the royal bones we share.